A Candlelight Ecstasy Romance

"YOU DON'T KNOW WHAT YOU WANT, RACHEL," BEN TOLD HER ANGRILY.

"The only commitment you're willing to make is to this farm. Well, so be it, but don't ask me to like it."

"I have no choice. It's the way it has to be. I'm not free like you to do whatever I please."

"What do you want me to say, Rachel? That I understand and it doesn't matter? That I'll finish out the season regardless of the friction between us?"

"It would ease my mind immensely," she admitted in a low voice.

He glared at her. "I'll stick it out on one condition."

"Which is?"

"That whatever I do on my personal time is none of your affair. I don't intend to hibernate on this farm until harvest." He paused. "Unlike you, I have other needs."

CANDLELIGHT ECSTASY CLASSIC ROMANCES

CANDLELIGHT ECSTASY ROMANCES®

SWEET TEMPEST

Eileen Bryan

A CANDLELIGHT ECSTASY ROMANCE®

Published by
Dell Publishing Co., Inc.
1 Dag Hammarskjold Plaza
New York, New York 10017

Dell ® TM 681510, Dell Publishing Co., Inc.

Candlelight Ecstasy Romance®, 1,203,540, is a registered trademark of Dell Publishing Co., Inc., New York, New York.

ISBN: 0-440-18310-3

Printed in the United States of America

November 1986

10 9 8 7 6 5 4 3 2 1

WFH

To Our Readers:

We have been delighted with your enthusiastic response to Candlelight Ecstasy Romances®, and we thank you for the interest you have shown in this exciting series.

In the upcoming months we will continue to present the distinctive sensuous love stories you have come to expect only from Ecstasy. We look forward to bringing you many more books from your favorite authors and also the very finest work from new authors of contemporary romantic fiction.

As always, we are striving to present the unique, absorbing love stories that you enjoy most—books that are more than ordinary romance. Your suggestions and comments are always welcome. Please write to us at the address below.

Sincerely,

The Editors
Candlelight Romances
1 Dag Hammarskjold Plaza
New York, New York 10017

SWEET
TEMPEST

CHAPTER ONE

"Dammit to hell!"

Thoroughly exasperated, Rachel Daniels gave up trying to pry loose the corroded battery cable of the pickup. Instead, she kicked at the tread-worn front tire disgustedly, as if that might coerce the obstinate truck's cooperation. But nothing she did seemed to have the slightest effect on the old Ford.

Tired and frustrated, she threw aside her pair of pliers with another unintelligible curse, and then slung her bibbed-overall-clad figure onto the ground. There she sat pouting with her legs crossed, her elbows propped upon her knees, and her suntanned cheeks pressed between her calloused palms. It was only when her daughter—a pert little three-foot-three-inch version of herself—reenacted to a tee the temper fit she'd thrown that Rachel realized how ridiculously childishly she had behaved. She glanced at the six-year-old girl, who had assumed a similar miffed posture beside her. In spite of her foul humor, a grudging grin broke upon her full lips.

"It's wrong to use curse words, Meggie," she reminded her.

"You did." Though only a few years out of diapers and barely into kindergarten, Margaret Jane Daniels could be highly independent and damnably observant at the most inopportune times.

"Well, I shouldn't have. I was just mad and acting badly." Idly, she smoothed Meggie's stubborn wheat-colored tresses. No matter how often Rachel brushed her daughter's hair, the locks stubbornly refused to stay in place. Like their owner, the spirited curls had a will of their own.

Meggie crooked her head and peered up at her mother with bright brown eyes. "Are we having a bad day?" She mimicked the words Rachel would often say to her when things weren't quite right in her little world.

Amused by Meggie's parroting, Rachel ruffed the mop of wild curls, correcting, "Not *we*, my love. Only mama is having a minor crisis, but I'm not going to let it get me down." She sprang to her feet, dusted off the seat of her overalls, then swung Meggie up into her arms. "If you're not careful, you'll miss the school bus. Or are you daw-dling on purpose again, Margaret Jane Daniels?" she asked, walking down the lane toward black-topped Farm Road.

"I hate school." Instantly, Meggie's expression changed from all smiles to a frown. "It's dumb, and Mrs. Lawrence smells like broccoli." Broccoli was Meggie's least favorite vegetable and, in her mind, an apt metaphor for her teacher. "Why do I have to go anyway? I want to stay with you." Her plump arms linked around Rachel's neck. Just as firmly, her white sneakers hooked around her mother's waist. Every day, Monday through Friday, they went through the same ordeal—Meggie balking and Rachel insisting that she board the bus for the rural ele-mentary school twenty miles away.

Wiping the traces of a milk moustache from Meggie's upper lip, Rachel unraveled herself from the tot's clutches and set her down. "We've been through this all before. I don't intend to explain it many more times, Meggie. You must go to school. It's what children do. Getting an education is a necessary thing so that you can grow up to be a smart young woman."

"I don't wanna be a smart young woman," Meggie whined. "I told you"—she kicked the dirt impatiently—"I wanna be just a plain old mama like you."

Though the remark was hardly flattering, Rachel knew her daughter meant it as a compliment of the highest sort. "Nonetheless, I'm afraid you're still going to have to attend school for another few years at least." A timely reprieve presented itself as the familiar yellow school bus came into view. "Have you got your snack and milk money?"

Head bent dejectedly, eyes downcast, Meggie nodded.

"Can I have a good-bye kiss?" Rachel stooped and presented her cheek as the bus ground to a halt before their modest farm.

"Nope. Meggie's mad and acting badly." Referring to herself in the third person as her mother had done earlier, she abruptly pivoted on the balls of her tennies and prepared to make a haughty retreat. Much to her chagrin, she wasn't quite quick enough. Rachel managed to plant a love tap on her fanny as she climbed aboard. The doors wheezed shut, and the lumbering bus began a slow tug up the road. Rachel waited, knowing full well that Meggie would skedaddle to the rear window in order to give her a parting gesture. Predictably, Meggie's freckled face appeared, nose pressed flat against the glass as she gave the secret "yuk" sign—crossing her eyes and sticking out her tongue.

Lord knew Meggie needed no encouragement when it came to rascality, yet she was like a ray of sunshine in

11

Rachel's bleak life. She laughed at her daughter's antics before strolling back to her troubles. The out-of-commission pickup was only one small disaster in a seemingly endless siege of hard times and bad luck. The damned truck had quit running last night, but she had been too tired to deal with it then. Actually, she was too weary and too beset even to deal with such simple tasks as going into Lubbock to grocery shop or making a dental appointment. Soon she would have to, though, since the freezer was nearly bare and an annoying cavity in a back molar was becoming a very real pain. But who had the time? Up at daybreak, working a struggling farm to try to stave off foreclosure, raising a spirited child, taking care of incidental household chores, running errands, and falling a little more behind each day until dropping exhaustedly into bed after a much-needed bath—this was her lot, her life now.

Rachel Daniels tried not to feel sorry for herself as she approached her most recent setback—the dead pickup. Unless she got the old heap running, they'd be marooned without a means to pay for either a wrecker or a mechanic's fee. Christ! What else could happen? she wondered. She couldn't face another bout with the contrary Ford just yet. She decided to indulge herself and have a second cup of coffee this morning. Maybe she'd just sit on the stoop and stare into space for a few divine, recuperative minutes. Do nothing. Worry about nothing. Merely look out over the flat South Plains, listen to the wind whine, and visualize a bumper crop of prime cotton—which would make a welcome relief from the hardships of late.

Hands thrust deep into the pockets of her overalls, she trudged across the neglected yard to the two-story frame house that showed signs of weathering. It desperately needed a fresh coat of paint, not to mention a new roof.

She forced herself not to think about such repairs. It did no good since she could not afford either the supplies or the time. First things first. Surviving the creditors and another harsh winter claimed top priority this planting season.

Blanking everything else from her mind, Rachel hurried inside the rambling kitchen, filled a mug with strong coffee, then returned to the sprawling porch and perched herself on the railing. She dangled a long leg, leaned her sun-streaked head back against a corner post, closed her eyes, and savored the few precious minutes of serene solitude. A gusty breeze ruffled the wisps of hair that escaped from beneath the blue bandanna tied around her forehead. The kerchief had become as second nature to her as the plain gold wedding band she still wore. Though Yancy had been dead for almost a full year, the ring he had placed upon her finger eight years ago had yet to be forsaken. Unconsciously, her thumb rubbed across the dainty gold band while her mind wandered.

Eyes shut, she could visualize Yancy as he'd been in the early years—tall, tawny, and full of the devil. He'd made her laugh then. Oh yes, in the beginning, he had the ability to make light of life and make love as if it were a brand new experience each and every time they lay together. She did sorely miss him at times. Even after the bitter years and quarrels, even after he'd lost his initiative and grit and become more attached to hard liquor than honest work, even after he'd mortgaged the farm to the hilt during the real estate boom of 1980 in order to buy additional acreage, which ultimately he left lying idle, even after he brought them to the brink of disaster without assuming the blame or confiding the circumstances, even after the drunken fool fell asleep behind the wheel and careened into an eighteen-wheeler on his way home from Lubbock, leaving her a widow at thirty with staggering funeral expenses and no insurance, she still occasionally pined for him. Maybe she mourned how he used to be. At other times, she cursed him for leaving her in such dire straits.

Rachel opened her almond-colored eyes to the reality of her present situation—the fallow fields, the deteriorating buildings and equipment, the unmended fencing, the past-due notices from the South Plains Farmers Exchange and McMurtry's Seed and Supplies stacked on the kitchen counter. And now there was the confounded pickup! She brought the mug to her mouth, sipping the strong brew and mulling over her present dismal state. Sometimes when she thought about Yancy's recklessness and negligence, she wished he'd come back to life so she could kill him herself, especially when she remembered his insistence long ago that she not criticize or interfere with *his* running of *her* family farm.

"For God's sake, Rachel. Give me credit for a little sense, will ya?" he had ranted. "You know nothing about the economics of farming. It's a business, not a damned homestead. And it's irritating as hell for you to keep hounding me about every petty detail. Either you got faith in me or you don't. Either I wear the pants in this family or you. Which is it to be?" he had challenged.

There had seemed to be only one way to salvage their strained marriage: assuage Yancy's wounded pride and not interfere in his administration of the farm. It had been a colossal mistake, as she discovered soon after his death. He'd even borrowed against his life insurance policy in an attempt to forestall the creditors.

Rachel swallowed another bitter gulp, just as she'd swallowed her pride when she had begged an extension on the mortgage note due at the first of the year. Now it was May and planting time, and Hershell Beck, the loan officer over at the South Plains Farmers Exchange, was growing impatient. If she could just keep that vulture at bay for a little longer—just until harvest time . . . If the good Lord would just look with favor on her and make it a mild season so the cotton would be high-grade . . . If the damned price would go up . . . If she didn't collapse from sheer exhaustion. Perhaps then the farm could be back on solid footing, and she and Meggie could finally be secure.

She slung the bottom dredge of coffee grounds into the bushes, then stood and peered out over her land. She'd do it or die trying, she silently vowed. Rachel Hobson Daniels wasn't going to accept foreclosure and the sale of her daughter's heritage without a dandy fight. Oh sure, she'd been advised to sell out for what she could auction. She'd been told by the male population of Mesquite Junction that a woman didn't stand much of a chance when it came to running a farm alone. Well, she'd been fool enough to listen to a male ego once before. This time, she'd do it her way. Better to fight and fail than to blindly accept and regret. At least she'd have control and a final say over her situation. This was one widow who'd learned the hard way to rely on herself.

Shading her eyes, Rachel noted the angle of the sun in the sky. Gracious! How long had she been sitting and dwelling on the past? Silently she reproached herself for wallowing in self-pity when so much needed to be done. Depositing the empty mug on the window sill, she mentally charged herself to do battle with the pickup. "Okay, you cantankerous old piece of junk. Let's tangle," she said out loud. Resolve glinting in her eyes, she strode purposefully across the yard, reclaimed the pliers, and began prying at the corroded cable once more. This time the seal broke free, allowing her to scrape, then squeeze the conductive clamps tighter, in the hope of producing a positive connection.

Out of habit she scratched her nose with the back of her hand, forgetting the grime and leaving a black smudge on the tip of her nose. "You'd better start, or I swear I'll sell you for scrap the first chance I get." Slinging open the door, she climbed into the cab of the truck and arranged herself behind the wheel. It was when she was making a motion to start the engine that she hesitated: a glimpse of a ropelike object lying coiled on the passenger side of the floorboard diverted her attention. She blinked, refocused, and froze when she finally identified the distraction.

A Snake. A silent alarm blared in her brain and sent chills up her spine. The only muscle still functioning in her body was her heart, and it was beating double time. Not many things frightened Rachel. Once she'd even fended off a rabid dog with a broom when it had trespassed onto her property and threatened Meggie, who was sunbathing in her playpen. But snakes were another story. Ever since she'd been a child, she'd had a phobia about them. And here she was trapped in a pickup with what appeared to be the biggest damned rattler in West Texas.

Though the windows were open, she could hardly breathe. Yancy's white T-shirt beneath her overalls clung like a second skin to her perspiring body. If she made the slightest move, it might strike. If she sat like a hypnotized bird, her chances weren't much better. Dear God! What should she do? If she didn't take some course of action soon, she'd drop dead of cardiac arrest.

She felt a sneeze coming on. Sheer instinct brought the back of her hand to her nose to smother the involuntary impulse. The rattler's coil tightened at the movement. Rachel tensed, too. It was a standoff between the rattler and the widow—the snake was waiting for her to make another minuscule motion, and she was sitting stone still and praying it would choose to slither off.

"Have ya got kin in Mesquite Junction, or are ya just passing through?" Bubba Atkins slanted a curious look across the breadth of the pickup at the hitchhiker he'd just picked up on the outskirts of Lubbock.

Bennett Eaton pulled the Stetson lower over his eyes so as to hide their amused glimmer. He strongly suspected that none of the relatives of the people who lived in this small community had migrated beyond a fifty-mile radius, and that they were well known to the locals. And why in the name of heaven would any outsider linger any longer than it took to earn enough to move on? "The latter," he replied disinterestedly.

"I figured as much." Bubba turned and spat his tobacco juice out the opened window. "Hardly anybody comes here on purpose, except for a few farm equipment salesmen and the Reverend Gabriel Walker when he holds his annual autumn revival."

"I guess that's quite an event." Having little else to occupy him at the moment, Ben decided that chatting with the old man beat the heck out of merely staring at the monotonous landscape.

"Yeah, it stirs us up a bit." Bubba chuckled. "The missus thinks he's John the Baptist reincarnated. We have an eleventh commandment around our house: Thou shalt not miss the Reverend Walker's Christian crusade."

A slow smile spread across Ben's face, but he declined any further comment on the subject of evangelism. "This is cotton country, isn't it?"

17

"Mainly, but we grow winter wheat and sorghum, too. Ya know much about farming?" Bubba veered sharply left to keep from hitting a runaway chicken strutting onto the road.

"Some" was the spare reply. There ensued a pause before Ben offered, "My grandparents had a farm in Iowa. I used to visit as a boy."

"Mmm," Bubba mumbled, not very impressed with the credentials. "Had business in Lubbock, did ya?" he pried.

"Nothing permanent. I move around a lot these days." Every trace of smile faded, and Ben shifted uneasily.

Being observant, Bubba noted the stranger's fidgeting. "What's your trade?"

"Nowadays, I suppose you could say that I'm a jack of all." Ben averted his gaze to the fields once more. "Would you happen to know if anyone is interested in hiring extra help around here?"

The question caught Bubba off guard. He assessed the hitchhiker. He didn't look like an ordinary migrant—too urban. Although his clothes were nothing fancy and were noticeably faded and although he talked down-to-earth, he had an air about him. Nope, he wasn't just another cotton picker or wheat rat.

"Well, let's see." Bubba mulled the prospects over for a second or two. "Only one I know of who could probably use some help is the widow Daniels. 'Course, she's gotten real peculiar lately. Stays out there on that farm and does nothing but work from dawn to dusk. Don't socialize a'tall anymore, except to attend Sunday services. Even then she don't chat much. Shame, too. She used to be a friendly sort before Yancy killed hisself."

"Suicide?"

"Got drunk and piled into an eighteen-wheeler hauling

18

hogs. Pret' near the same thing, I expect," Bubba explained.

"How big a place does she have?" Ben wanted to ascertain if the widow Daniels truly could provide enough work to stake him to his next stopover.

" 'Bout four hundred acres or so. But only half of it is fit for planting. The rest ain't cleared and is running over with mesquite. Yancy didn't much put his heart or back into farming—not the way he did into booze and Marybeth Waylon. She tends bar at an icehouse between Acuff and Lubbock that Yancy used to frequent. 'Course, I don't believe Rachel knew about her. Probably for the best," the old man said in a sympathetic postscript.

Ben really preferred to skip the gossip. "Is the Daniels place far from here?"

Bubba applied the brakes and eased the pickup onto the shoulder of the road. "We just passed it. It's right over yonder." He pointed to the property on his left. "Ya getting off or going on?"

Ben Eaton reached for the duffel bag tucked between his cramped legs. "I think I'll pay my respects to the widow and see if she's in need of some help. I appreciate the lift" was his cordial reply as he got out of the pickup.

Bubba leaned across the seat, his tone good-natured as he warned, "I wouldn't put much stock in her hiring ya. I forgot to mention that Rachel's got a reputation for being tight these days. Might not be another ride come along for hours. Sure you wanna dally here?"

"I'll take my chances." Ben touched the brim of his Stetson and stepped back dismissingly.

"Okay. It's your time and shoe leather, I reckon. So long," Bubba bade him.

Ben removed the Stetson, shading his eyes from the glare of the spring sun and surveying the Daniels farm.

19

Judging by the condition of the place, the widow could use an extra pair of hands, all right. And judging by the condition of his finances and the growl of his empty stomach, he most definitely wouldn't be too proud to do manual labor for fair wages. He caught a firmer grip on the duffel bag, then proceeded on up to the house and knocked on the screen door. He received no answer except for the incessant barking of a dog from inside, but the place looked as if someone were on the grounds—the front door stood wide open and a radio was playing.

Deciding that the widow was more than likely occupied out back, he dropped his bag onto the porch and headed in the direction of the barn. He hadn't covered more than a hundred yards or so when he spied an old pickup parked beside the rickety structure and what appeared to be the figure of a woman behind the wheel.

"Excuse me for bothering you, ma'am," he called out. "The name's Ben Eaton." He doffed the Stetson from off his head respectfully. The woman's only acknowledgment of him was a brusque cut of her eyes. Bubba had been right: the widow Daniels was strange. He stepped closer. "One of your neighbors mentioned you might be in need of some help, and—"

"At the moment that's an understatement." The queer remark was spoken in a low, raspy voice. "Please come over to the truck, but walk easy, mister."

Her odd behavior made him slightly leery, but he did as she requested.

Near hysteria, Rachel fought to keep her composure. The man was a godsend, but she knew that any premature display of jubilation on her part could very well incite the snake. Difficult as it was, she held herself in check until the stranger was near enough to be apprised of her dilemma. Then, as calmly and succinctly as possible, she merely said, "I'm penned up in this pickup with a rattler." At the stunned disbelief that registered on the stranger's face, she gestured to the motionless snake lying on the floorboard with a barely perceptible quirk of her head. "I'm open to suggestions, mister," she entreated.

In his thirty-four years, Ben Eaton had heard and seen his share of the bizarre and had taken charge in many a crisis situation, but the one in which he found himself at present was absolutely the damnedest predicament he'd ever encountered. "Holy sh—"

"My sentiments exactly," Rachel agreed.

"How the devil are we going to get you out of there without antagonizing it?" He glanced around as if an answer might materialize out of thin air.

Her nerves strained to the point of snapping, Rachel spoke through gritted teeth. "Hell! If I could have figured out a solution to that, I wouldn't be asking for a second opinion. Will you please do something quick before I pass smooth out?"

Realizing how terrified she must be, Ben took no offense at her surly comeback. "Don't panic." His steady hand curved around the door handle. "And try not to pass out in the next second or two." His voice was reassuring as his thumb eased in the button. "Okay, here goes," he forewarned a split second before he lurched open the door, grabbed her roughly by the arm, and wrenched her from the cab. The cry of protest she would've uttered became instead a groan as she landed in the dirt.

Lightning fast, he slammed the door shut on the striking rattler. "Come on," he urged, hauling her onto her feet. "Let's get clear in case that damned thing decides to crawl out the window. God! I hate snakes. They scare the daylights out of me."

21

Half dazed, she allowed him to pull her, stumbling, to an elm tree a safe distance away. But no sooner did it dawn on her that she was out of harm's way than the aftershock of her ordeal set in. Suddenly, her knees grew weak and a smothering sensation overcame her. She braced her backside against the stout tree trunk and bent to gasp.

"You're hyperventilating. Concentrate on taking slow, deep breaths." Ben observed her closely, but he offered no further assistance.

For some absurd reason, his unruffled tone and concise diagnosis grated on her. Once she'd managed to regain herself, she straightened and inspected him with a cool look. In all the excitement, she'd failed to notice anything more than generalities about her savior. Now that she had an opportunity to study him in detail, she realized what a striking figure he cut—commandingly tall, superbly toned, and incredibly tanned. His features were not exactly what one would call dashing, for there lurked a hint of ruggedness beneath the surface: the square cut of his chin, the sharp clarity of his eyes, the noble-looking, straight-bridged nose. The fine lines etched at the corners of his eyes and between his brows were the mark of a man who'd looked into many a bright horizon and had had more than once been scored by the trials of life. Were she studying Greek literature rather than contemplating a jean-clad stranger, she would have thought of him as a Spartan personified, such was the image he conjured, the magnetism he generated.

"What did you say your name was?" She tucked her hands into her hip pockets, trying to nullify his effect on her by reacting with only the vaguest interest.

"Eaton," he replied. "Ben Eaton."

"I appreciate the rescue, Mr. Eaton. Now tell me,

which good-intentioned neighbor of mine led you to believe that I had work to hire out?" A hint of annoyance colored her voice.

In some ways the widow was as peculiar as Bubba had warned, yet she wasn't exactly what Ben had expected to find. She was much younger and definitely prettier but was regrettably about as sociable as the rattler. "I don't remember the man's name. Just someone who gave me a lift out of Lubbock." He offered no further details, sensing that he might have good reason to protect Bubba's identity.

Her aloof almond eyes studied him. "Have you any experience on a farm?" she finally asked.

"I've enough to help plant your crop and do some general maintenance around here."

The quiet confidence he exuded stirred Rachel's curiosity. Mr. Eaton was unlike the numerous other drifters who'd solicited temporary work from her while passing through. His manner of speech and carriage was that of a man more inclined to issuing instructions than to doing another's bidding. Even his expression held a certain natural hauteur. She lowered her gaze, unable to maintain eye contact, and admitted, "Since I couldn't pay you what your labor would be worth, you'd do better to look elsewhere, Mr. Eaton."

Being no stranger to tough times himself, Ben appreciated the widow's candor. The tone of her voice and her inability to look him directly in the eye when declining assistance that she could obviously use told him a lot about her character. Although she was immensely proud, the widow was also refreshingly honest. She brought to mind a crisis season in his own life and how humbling the experience had been for him. He found himself wanting to lend her a helping hand, but he was at a loss as to how

23

to phrase his offer so that it wouldn't be interpreted as charity.

"I've been elsewhere, ma'am, and whatever you could pay is a better offer than I've received so far. If you're willing to provide meals and accommodations, I'm willing to wait until harvest time to collect my wages." The crazy proposition spilled from him before he'd given it proper consideration. Had he really committed himself to long, arduous months of hard labor out of a misguided sense of compassion for a struggling young widow? He must be suffering from sunstroke!

Rachel was as startled as he by the outlandish offer. She lifted her head and gazed directly into his kinetic hazel eyes. Many possible motives for his unorthodox proposal flitted through her mind, but that he had acted out of pity was simply not one of them. Her major reservation was the idea of taking a strange man into her home without even the slightest inkling as to his moral fiber. Yet she sensed that this man was neither riffraff nor an opportunist. Although he hadn't offered any references, it was evident by his polite manner that Ben Eaton possessed at least a passable degree of integrity. Instinctively, she trusted him—not entirely, but enough to give him a chance to prove or disprove her initial impression. "That would be an agreeable arrangement to me, Mr. Eaton. As long as you understand that there is always the possibility of a crop failure and that if there is, I wouldn't be able to reimburse your back wages."

"I'm aware of that, Miz Daniels. I'll risk it." He wondered why he didn't bow out of his own ridiculous proposition and walk away while he still had the opportunity.

"Well, then." The widow actually smiled, and Ben discovered himself mildly affected by the soft curve of her full lips and the appearance of two beguiling dimples at

24

the corners of her mouth. Although the widow Daniels wore no trace of makeup except for the smudge of grease on the tip of her bobbed nose, she was a comely woman. "I suppose we could best begin our arrangement with your disposing of the snake," she suggested.

Ben all but flinched. "It's probably crawled off into some hole by now." He prayed that it had.

Seemingly oblivious to his reluctance, she began to walk back toward the pickup. "Well, just in case it hasn't, there's a machete in the barn."

He followed her lead, still trying to think of some alternate recourse to doing hand-to-hand combat with the rattler. "I'd prefer a shotgun," he said in all seriousness.

Pivoting abruptly, Rachel nearly collided with her newly acquired hired hand. "Are you nuts? How much good do you think that old pickup will be to me after you blow a hole the size of a watermelon through it?"

Ben strongly considered posing an equally unsavory question to the headstrong widow: How much good would a snakebit paladin do her? Deciding it would be best not to begin their association by arguing with her, he merely asked, "If the snake is still nested in the pickup and I'm forced to kill it, what would you like me to do with the carcass?"

"Hack it to pieces and bury it deep enough that Napoleon won't dig it up" was her reply.

"Napoleon?" he said bewilderedly.

"Our dog," she explained.

"Our?" he repeated, confused by the plural reference.

"Mine and my daughter Meggie's. He's a Doberman. And now that you know the Daniels clan in detail, do you suppose you could tend to the snake, Mr. Eaton?"

Her curt tone, coupled with the impatient look she cast him, provoked Ben's usually temperate nature. It had been several years since a woman—or a particular situation—had gotten the better of him. "Hack it to pieces, huh?" He squared his broad shoulders, his smirk unmistakably patronizing. "Perhaps I should take a lesson from the rattler and make certain not to get crosswise with you."

"Perhaps you should." Her expression changed to one of stubbornness.

He touched the brim of his Stetson in mock obeisance, then retreated with one final comment: "And perhaps you should powder your nose, Miz Daniels. Unless it's your custom to use axle grease as makeup, that is." He sauntered off in the direction of the barn, leaving her mortified and, for the first time since they had met, speechless. She swiped a forearm across her out-of-joint nose.

CHAPTER TWO

Much to Ben's dismay, the cursed snake was still staking squatter's rights in the pickup. If he weren't trying to prove a point to the feisty widow, he'd just as soon let the reptile sunbathe undisturbed until it decided to leave of its own accord. But Miz Daniels had decreed that the damned thing be drawn and quartered as punishment for daring to trespass on her space, and the executioner had no choice but to comply or admit cowardice. Ben Eaton was braver and more resourceful than most men, but he truly loathed snakes. Nonetheless, he managed to muster enough courage to sever the snake's head before its venomous strike pierced anything more vulnerable than his boot leather.

He was shoveling a last spadeful of dirt over the mutilated remains when a breathy little voice asked, "Whatcha doing?" He turned to face a cherub-faced girl who had the same disarming dimples as her mother.

"You must be Meggie," he greeted, resting the spade against the barn door and wiping his hands on the back of his jeans.

"Sometimes I am," she said pertly. "Sometimes I'm Margaret Jane. And sometimes I'm invisible with no name a'tall." She sucked her Tootsie Pop and inspected the tall stranger.

Ben grinned broadly, charmed by her West Texas drawl and amused by her none-too-subtle scrutiny. "I'm Ben Eaton, and I'm pleased to make your acquaintance, ma'am." He extended a hand to the saucy miss.

Without the slightest hesitation, she placed her small hand in his. "I'm not a ma'am, silly," she giggled. "I'm a Meggie, just like you guessed."

From the moment of their introduction, a mutual rapport developed between Ben and Meggie. She shadowed him for the remainder of the afternoon, asking a hundred questions and divulging a personal history so detailed that she designated Ben her "very bestest friend." By the time Rachel summoned them to supper, Ben knew Meggie's favorite ice cream, her secret hiding spots, her dislike of broccoli, her love of Napoleon, her chicken pox scar (which she called "chicken pops"), her numerous fights with her tattletale friend Dory Phillips, her firm belief in extraterrestrials, her disgust with school, and her rifling of her mother's dresser drawer, where there lay a treasure of fancy lingerie to be plundered. The last confidence, although an intriguing sidelight on Miz Daniels's diamond-tough exterior, Ben wisely decided to treat as classified information. He doubted that the widow would be thrilled at the prospect of his being privy to her fetish for sheer, provocative bedroom apparel.

"Come on," Meggie urged, tugging at his hand. "If Mama has to whistle twice, we'll be in big trouble. Besides, we're having fried chicken tonight. It's yummy."

Meggie didn't have to repeat the endorsement, and Rachel didn't have to whistle twice. The memory of his grandmother's scrumptious fried chicken and mashed potatoes drenched in thick cream gravy made from the brownings whetted Ben's appetite. If there was one thing a person could rely on during a stint on a farm, it was delectable food. More years had passed then he cared to remember since he'd tasted anything that resembled home cooking. Perhaps, considering the fringe benefits, he hadn't made such a poor bargain after all. He raced Meggie to the back door, anticipating that long-forgotten smell of succulent chicken, deep fried to crispy perfection.

"Ben and I are making good friends, Mama," Meggie enthused, plopping herself down at the kitchen table. "I think we should become blood brothers, like Cory Thompson and Brodie Wallers did," she chattered.

"And I think you should wash your hands before we discuss it." Rachel snapped off the oven and finished pouring the iced tea.

"But I washed 'em after school," Meggie protested.

"I'm sure you did, but I insist that you do it once more." Rachel ignored Ben's presence as she placed the tea glasses on the table.

"Yes, ma'am" came the obedient whine as Meggie deserted them and trotted to the bathroom a short distance down the hall.

"Please, take a seat at the end of the table, Mr. Eaton." Rachel gestured at a chair, still not deigning to glance at him as she bustled about the spacious kitchen.

He sniffed the air in the hope of detecting the aroma he'd anticipated. Oddly, no such smell assailed his senses. His gaze swept the stove and countertops for the familiar cast iron skillet or a reasonable facsimile thereof. None was present. The widow was either the neatest cook he'd ever encountered or a magician. He wondered if she was planning to produce fried chicken like a rabbit out of a top hat. "If it won't delay supper, I need to wash up, too," he said distractedly.

As she bent to open the oven, he began to suspect the

29

worst. "TV dinners keep, Mr. Eaton. Take all the time you need" was her gracious reply.

The exasperated roll of Ben's eyes heavenward as he passed Meggie in the hall prompted a gleeful "Look, Mama! Ben can make the 'yuk' sign, too" from the tattling darling.

Ben had barely managed to cloister himself in the bathroom before he grumbled a colorful expletive. He threw cold water on his face in an attempt to ward off the slow burn welling within him. "TV dinners isn't exactly home cooking, is it, Eaton?" he muttered between splashes. "This is a helluva deal you've struck." Snatching a towel from the rack, he blotted his face, then studied his image in the mirror. Okay, so maybe cooking isn't one of the fringe benefits, he silently reasoned. Maybe after the snake incident, this is just an off night for her. At least you'll be sleeping in a comfy bed for a change. Even if a feather mattress isn't in your future, the accommodations have to be better than loud motel rooms and lumpy foam rubber. But he decided not to jump to conclusions as he joined the already-seated mother and daughter.

"See, Ben? I told you it was going to be yummy." Meggie flashed him a superior smile.

He glanced down at the divided aluminum foil plate, his stomach rebelling at the sight of soggy chicken, instant mashed potatoes, withered English peas, and an unidentifiable dessert. "Yummy," he agreed unenthusiastically.

"Mama makes us say the blessing before we eat." Meggie clamped her hands together and piously bent her curly head.

He followed her example, silently beseeching forgiveness for the wicked thought he was having: serving Miz Daniels dissected rattlesnake—raw.

Rachel covertly watched him from beneath lowered lashes. She could almost read his mind. The supper he'd expected was a far cry from what he'd received. Well, too damned bad. What did he think? That she had time to whip up fresh biscuits, Southern fried chicken, and deep-dish apple pie after working like a plow horse the livelong day? If he didn't like the menu, he could order pizza from Lubbock. Otherwise, he could eat what she offered and be grateful.

"God is great. God is good. Thank you, God, for our food. Amen," Meggie chirped.

"Amen" came the simultaneous grunt from opposite ends of the table.

Except for Meggie's occasional banter, they consumed the dinner in strained silence. Only a "pass the salt, please" or a curt "thank you" passed between the widow and her hired hand.

It didn't take Rachel long to tidy up, and in less than an hour she had Meggie bathed, powdered, tickled, kissed, and tucked in tight.

It was only when she returned to the kitchen and began the evening ritual she'd come to enjoy that she remembered Ben Eaton and her manners. She found him sitting on the back porch railing, staring into space and toting on a slim cheroot. The sight of his manly silhouette filled her with nostalgia, and for a fleeting moment she was lost in suppressed yearning—the kind of yearning that arouses sensuality. She caught herself teetering on the brink between illusion and reality, and she quickly looked away. His presence made her loneliness all the more acute, somehow. It bothered her, this strange melancholy that the drifter instilled. She couldn't understand the hostility she'd felt toward him throughout the day. After all, he'd practically saved her life, had generously

31

offered to hire on without a guarantee of payment for his services, and had been extraordinarily kind to Meggie. And in return she'd been less than hospitable. Why? she wondered. Why was she behaving as if he were a threat rather than a blessing?

She decided to make amends by inviting him to share in her evening toddy. Perhaps the simple courtesy might be a catalyst for conversation between them. After all, she really knew very little about the man who'd be sleeping under her roof.

She added a finishing touch of whipped cream to the toddies and strolled out onto the back porch. "I thought you might like to join me. Sometimes in the evening I treat myself to an Irish coffee and just sit out here looking at the stars." She passed him the peace offering and settled onto the porch steps.

"I haven't had one of these in a long time." He flicked the ashes on the cheroot and sipped the toddy, casting her a wary glance over the edge of the mug. The spiked coffee had a bite—kind of like the widow. "I'd almost forgotten how good these things were. Thank you," he said appreciatively.

"You're welcome" was the polite reply. Suddenly, making amiable small talk became difficult and she found herself struggling. "My husband introduced me to Irish coffee one weekend in Dallas. I've had a fondness for it ever since."

"For toddies or Dallas?" A slow grin materialized on his face as he watched her reaction.

The initial rebuke in her eyes diminished as she became intrigued by his smile. "Toddies," she clarified. "Though I like Dallas, too. It's a nice town. Ever been there?"

The grin evaporated from his lips, and his gaze drifted into the distance. "I spent a good portion of my life in

32

Dallas. My impression of it is a bit different from yours. Then again, I guess it's no better or worse than any other place."

She wondered if she only imagined the cynicism in his voice. Something warned her that Dallas was a part of his life not open to discussion. "It's pleasant out here in the evening. At the end of a hectic day, I like to enjoy the peace and solitude."

His gaze fell on the widow, and he analytically observed her moonlit profile. It was a defined profile and yet also a delicate one. He could see both pride and strife in her face. She removed her bandanna and shook loose her hair. The freed strands petaled around her face, softening her features and making her appear younger and more vulnerable. "I'm sure you find the quiet restoring. You have a lot on your shoulders, Miz Daniels."

"That I do, Mr. Eaton."

He could almost hear her sigh.

She sipped the Irish coffee for a second or two, then set aside the mug, linked her hands around a knee, and leaned back, contemplating the onyx sky. "I strongly suspect that you've done a lot of drifting. Am I right?"

He took a swig of the spiked coffee, flipped the cheroot into the yard, and replied in the affirmative. "Yes, ma'am. In the last three years, I've traveled a lot."

She nodded at the confirmation. "In that respect, we're very different. All I know is this small corner of the world. It probably doesn't seem like much to most. I'm sure a majority of folks would wonder why I even bother to hang on to it. It's flat. The wind hardly ever lets up. It rains either too much or not enough. Then there's always the threat of hail and sand storms, tornadoes, and bitter winters. But with all its drawbacks, this land is what I know, and cotton is what I grow. I got a flair for it, like

33

some folks have a knack for politics or a head for business. Meggie and this land put meaning into my life. Maybe she won't give a tinker's damn about it when she grows up, but I'd like her to at least have the choice. Do you understand what I'm saying, Mr. Eaton?" She turned to him, curious to see from his expression if he related at all to what she'd confided.

He'd been listening intently and had been touched deeply. Although the widow had no way of knowing it, Ben Eaton was a man who'd already experienced the pain of losing the meaning in his life. He, better than most, could appreciate her determination to cling to her roots. "Your small corner of the world is as important as any other. I don't blame you at all for fighting to retain it."

She could tell by his sincere tone that her words had not been wasted. "The only reason I mentioned it is that I realize I can be unreasonable at times." She sipped from the mug, then smiled ruefully. "Even fanatical, on occasion. I drive myself hard, and I tend to forget that no one else has the same stake in the outcome as I do. I can be impatient, bad-tempered, and willful. Since you're bound to be seeing me at my worst, I thought it only fair to forewarn you."

He stood, stretching nonchalantly, then offering her an assisting hand up from the steps. "I'm not easily intimidated, Miz Daniels. Actually, I find a willful woman refreshing."

For some crazy reason, a lump came into her throat. There was a lulling quality about Ben Eaton—something reassuring and sensitive. Although she hadn't the slightest doubt that he was every bit as strong-minded as she, he possessed a worldliness, a certain maturity, that had nothing to do with age and everything to do with insight into human nature. His touch, however, was not so soothing. In fact, it was arousing—gentle yet possessive. She found it impossible to look at him while extricating her hand from his. "It's getting late. I'll show you where you'll be sleeping."

She disappeared inside, leaving him stranded on the porch and more than a little curious at her abrupt change of mood. Again he recalled Bubba's description of her. Peculiar, the old man had called her. In a sense she was: Peculiarly forthright. Peculiarly fundamental. And peculiarly attractive in an earthy sort of way.

"Coming, Mr. Eaton?"

The sound of her voice reclaimed his wandering thoughts. It had been a long day, and the prospect of a good night's sleep enticed him to follow the widow.

"This is a small community," she was saying, leading the way down the hall. "People thrive on gossip around here." More intent on a comfy bed than on her meaning, he only half paid attention. "So I think it's better for the sake of both our reputations not to give my neighbors any excuse to wag their tongues." She reached her destination —a door at the end of the hall—and apologized as she swung it open. "I'm sorry. I know it's cramped, but it's the best I can do. Separate floors will look less compromising than separate bedrooms."

Disbelievingly, his gaze swept the interior of the room. It wasn't much bigger than a broom closet.

"It used to be a storage area. It's clean. I worked all afternoon fixing it up."

A rollaway bed took up three-fourths of the allotted space. He could only imagine the quality of the mattress.

"I aired the feather mattress. It's comfortable, I can assure you," she went on.

Thank God for small favors, he silently mused.

"You'll have to leave the door open, of course." At his

35

befuddled look, she explained. "There's no window. You'll need ventilation. I put a small oscillating fan over in the corner in case you get too warm. Oh, and I made room for your things in the hall closet. There's even a small chest for your socks and such." She was trying so hard to convince him that the accommodations were more livable than appearances made them seem. "The bathroom's convenient—right across the hall."

"That's handy," he muttered, unable to keep the sarcasm from seeping through.

"Well, then. If there's nothing else I can get you . . ." She left the sentence dangling.

A shoehorn to wedge myself out of this squeeze-box in the morning would be nice, he thought to himself. "I'll manage" was his only response.

Her meek nod was the first sign of uncertainty she'd displayed. Halfway up the staircase, she paused, then leaned over the bannister to interject an afterthought. "Oh, I forgot to tell you about Napoleon. He has an attachment for that old rollaway, and he might seek it out in the middle of the night. Just shove him off. He's half blind from cataracts and lame with arthritis, but he's docile as a lamb. I ought to have him put to sleep, but Meggie adores him. I hope he doesn't disturb you, Mr. Eaton."

"Good night, Miz Daniels." He managed to keep his tone civil. Not until he heard the click of her bedroom door did he expel the curse he'd been suppressing. Since the room was hardly big enough to turn around in, he stripped in the hall before stepping into his cubbyhole and slinging his clothes into a corner.

Although sleeping on the feather mattress was like sleeping on a cloud, Ben was hot and restless. He tossed and turned, cursed, and punched the pillow repeatedly.

36

For the life of him he couldn't figure out why he'd volunteered his services to the widow. What was it about Rachel Daniels that had compelled him to put her interests before his own? In retrospect, his behavior had been totally out of character. Once upon a time her struggle to salvage a rundown farm wouldn't have affected him beyond a perfunctory observation such as "too bad" or "a damned shame." Even after he himself had become a recipient of similar observations, he'd been too numb, too estranged from his fellow man, to notice, let alone empathize with, anyone else's misfortune.

Only recently had he begun to rejoin the human race, to feel the desperation of those who were the ill-fated targets of life's unfairness. There was something about Rachel Daniels that aroused his conscience and rekindled a spark of belief. Perhaps it was nothing more than the pride he'd detected when she'd explained why she couldn't hire him. There was nothing covert or manipulative about her—no bitterness, no self-pity. She'd said very little, and yet she'd expressed volumes. Although they were as dissimilar as night and day, paradoxically, they were also kindred spirits. To have turned his back on her in her hour of need would have been to disclaim his own past, as if it had never occurred and had no significance. He couldn't do that. There had to be some purpose to his downfall, some lesson, some benefit.

The unmistakable sound of paw-pats on the hardwood floor alerted Ben. He rolled over and faced a pair of eerie amber eyes glowering at him out of the darkness. "Sorry, bub, but the bed's taken," he muttered drowsily.

Napoleon paid him no heed. With one giant leap he asserted his indisputable claim to the bed and sprawled across the breadth of it.

Taking Rachel at her word that the aged Doberman

37

had a mild disposition, Ben gave him a firm shove. In return, he received a lethal snarl and a flash of white teeth. Napoleon had no intention of vacating the bed. Ben considered himself lucky that the Doberman had no objection to sharing it. "Terrific. I'll bet the damned mutt snores, too," he seethed, drawing up his knees so as not to encroach on Napoleon's sovereign domain. Ben's hunch proved to be correct. In minutes, Napoleon was fast asleep and snoring louder than a drunken sailor.

Upstairs in her bedroom, Rachel inched closer to the mirror and critically examined her reflection. Goodness, but her skin was weathering. Why hadn't she noticed the dryness and those faint creases at the corners of her eyes before? She stepped back and surveyed herself from a less-revealing distance. At least the body beneath the filmy peach-colored nightgown was still firm and curvy in all the right places. Hard work had its advantages, she supposed.

Yet it bothered her that she'd not detected the lines around her eyes previously. When had they appeared? She presumed it had happened sometime after Yancy's death and before her thirtieth birthday. Grief and worry had obviously taken their toll. While Yancy was alive, she had seldom bothered to review herself. He thought her pretty, and she accepted the complimentary reflection in his admiring eyes. After his accident, she'd been too harried and had had no incentive to take account of her femininity. Why, suddenly, was she concerned about her appearance? Why was she taking stock of her womanly assets and liabilities tonight?

Angered by her foolish vanity, she turned from the mirror and crawled into bed, lying stiff as a board with the sheet tucked tightly under her chin. She was acting as silly as Desiree Sayer, fretting over a few wrinkles and primping like a schoolgirl. Never, ever would she allow herself to behave as asininely as the featherheaded, sex-hungry divorcee who flirted outrageously with every man in the county. She had more than enough to concern herself with without worrying about some man's opinion of her.

She'd never been the type that craved male attention. A drifter had happened along, and she'd caught a whiff of a manly scent, and because she'd been deprived of sex for quite some time, her hormones were a bit scrambled by his presence. But she had better sense than to accord him any more importance than was his due. He was just another drifter, and it was just another season in her life. By fall, the cotton would be harvested, and he'd be gone. Neither she nor her routine existence would be much altered by his temporary layover in Mesquite Junction.

Her grip on the sheet relaxed at having satisfactorily put Ben Eaton in perspective, and she gradually fell asleep.

CHAPTER THREE

But during the following weeks, Rachel had difficulty dismissing Ben Eaton as a minor part of her life. The drifter was making a major contribution toward revitalizing the failing farm. Moreover, try as she might, she could not help but occasionally notice that he was an extraordinarily good-looking man. At the oddest moments she'd be struck by the way the sunlight gleamed on his light brown hair or by the unexpected flash of his hazel eyes. He had a presence about him—a distinctive signature, so to speak. Although his gait was easy and his inflection was mild, a subtle prowess lurked beneath his casual demeanor. Rachel instinctively sensed that the man was as shrewd and potentially as fierce as he was lithe.

And if she had any doubts about the qualities she ascribed to him, they were dispelled whenever he removed his shirt. Never had she seen such a magnificently toned anatomy. It was at those particular times that her hormones would overload her rational circuits and cause her to fantasize things that even Desiree Sayer would consider risque. It was also at those agitated moments that she would attack whatever project she was in the midst of with excessive vigor while admonishing herself for having given in to such preposterous impulses.

Once, and only once, had Ben witnessed one of her

exorcizing fits. He had approached her as she was wrestling fifty-pound bags of seed from off the back of the pickup. "That's too heavy. Let me do it," he'd offered, coming up behind her and reaching around to confiscate the sack. His half-naked nearness and musky scent had made her more skittish than a high-strung Thoroughbred. "Thank you, but I'm accustomed to hard work, Mr. Eaton," she'd snapped. "Believe it or not, I managed just fine before you happened along." He'd backed off, just as she'd intended. Later, after regaining her objectivity, she'd felt duly repentant and had apologized to Ben for her outburst. He'd accepted her lame excuse of being out of sorts because of a headache, and the incident had been forgotten.

Actually, for the most part, they got along quite well, considering that they inescapably spent almost sixteen out of every twenty-four hours in nearly exclusive company. More often than not, Rachel was truly grateful for Meggie's intermittent presence. Her innocent mischief and unpredictable remarks eased the tension that now and then surfaced between herself and Ben because of their constant contact. Those who have no exposure to farming do not understand what an intimate thing it is for two people to work the land together. Plowing the earth and sowing the seed, keeping a watch on the sky and a guard on the field, sweating and cursing, aching and praying, celebrating the first eruption of a cotton plant through the brown turf and commiserating over the umpteenth breakdown of the cultivator—this is a sharing that no one else except those who rely on Mother Earth and each other can comprehend. In a sense, it is a communion of faith and discipline that belongs only to a special sect. And, oh, yes, it is an intimate thing—almost as personal and binding as an act of physical love.

With each day that passed, Ben appreciated more the gratification that comes from being in touch with nature —literally in touch. Although farming was harder work than he'd ever imagined, there was an essence of freedom about it, a sense of accomplishment. He derived great satisfaction from reshaping the lay of the land and coaxing the cotton crop along. It was like nothing he'd ever experienced before. In the past, Bennett Earl Eaton III had achieved with his sharp mind, not with his strong back. He'd accrued power and wealth through shrewd speculation and accelerated dealings. Now he patiently tended seedling cotton plants with a sluggish tractor. It was quite a change, but he'd had three years in which to make a gradual adjustment. No longer did he think in terms of setting the world on fire; no longer did he expect fast results or shows of respect. As for divine mercy and mortal loyalty, he'd long since decided that neither existed.

In those three years, the former-corporate-magnate-turned-drifter had grown to accept the collapse of his financial empire. Ever so slowly, his bitterness had become apathy, and then his apathy had finally changed to acceptance. Out of all those who had forsaken him during his crisis—God, family, friends, and business associates—there remained only two whom he had yet to forgive: one was the Almighty, and the other was his ex-wife. For a long time after his bankruptcy and subsequent divorce, Ben had had no tolerance either for women or for places of worship. In the last year or so, his attitude toward the female gender had mellowed somewhat, but he still refused to set foot inside a church.

His aversion to church had become a source of contention in the Daniels household. The widow held strong Christian convictions. She expected attendance at Sunday services, and she honored the commandment that prohibited doing labor on the Sabbath. For nearly a month of Sundays they'd bickered over both religious practices.

"This is ridiculous. All I want to do is mend a damned fence. It's *my* sweat and *my* soul," he'd protest.

"And it's *my* belief and *my* farm," she'd remind him.

"God isn't going to work miracles around here, Rachel. There's just you and I, and each week we fall another day behind."

"I'm tolerant of your irreverence. The least you can do is be respectful of my religious beliefs. I don't expect miracles, but I do have faith. And for goodness' sake, will you please refrain from running around like a half-naked heathen on Sundays?" At that time, his only sin had been wearing a shirt unbuttoned.

Meggie, too, was truly concerned about Ben's soul. Ever since overhearing the argument that had occurred between her mother and Ben the previous Sunday, she'd taken it upon her own small shoulders to save him from the devil's clutches before church services next week. Her powers of persuasion were much stronger than Rachel's. At bedtime on Saturday night, for the first time ever, Meggie climbed up into Ben's lap and hugged his neck. Rachel was curious as to her intent. Ben was totally enchanted and already a convert, although he'd yet to realize it.

"Won't you please come to church with us tomorrow, Ben?" Meggie pleaded. "I'm afraid for you. If you don't let God know that you're here with us in Mesquite Junction, he won't know where to find you. And if you should die before you wake, the devil will get you. And if the devil gets you, he'll take you to hell." She shivered at the thought and cuddled closer to him, burying her curly head in the crook of his neck and squeezing him tighter.

"It's an awful, awful place, Ben. Please, you just gotta come. If you sit beside me, I'll hold your hand and it won't be so bad."

He looked over at Rachel bewilderedly. She shrugged her shoulders. He considered telling Meggie the truth—that he'd experienced hell on earth and had no more fear of it—but quickly rejected that option.

"I might go just this once so God will have my address," he assured her with a loving pat.

Meggie appeared to be appeased for the moment. She kissed him soundly on the cheek, then wriggled from his lap, issuing directives like a seasoned coach. "You can't wear bluejeans. God doesn't like 'em. And you gotta be ready on time. Mama doesn't like to be late. 'Nighty-night, Ben."

As soon as Meggie had pitter-pattered up the stairs, Rachel pulled up a kitchen chair and expelled a deep sigh. "You do realize that she's manipulating you." From his astonished expression, the widow saw that he had had no inkling of Meggie's childish ploy.

"If by attending one Sunday service I'll ease her mind about my wayward soul, I can't refuse her. Sometimes you're too hard on her, Rachel. She's as close to an angel as I'll ever see."

"I'm telling you, she won't be content with only one Sunday. Margaret Jane has every intention of making a convert out of you. She knows exactly how to wrap you around her little finger."

"She's the first female in quite a while who could," he said absently.

Rachel caught the unintended slip, but she wisely let it pass, at least temporarily. "Don't say I didn't warn you. Join me in an Irish coffee?" she offered.

He nodded, easing back into his chair and watching

44

her go through the motions of the ritual. Lately, he'd been observing her whenever the opportunity presented itself. Oddly, he'd also been remembering Meggie's divulgence that Rachel's dresser drawer was full of filmy lingerie. He remembered this especially on Sundays, when Rachel donned a dress and discarded the ever-present bandanna. Miz Daniels was a very pretty woman who had a perfectly proportioned and exceptionally fit body. The crazy thing was, she had no conception of how attractive a woman she was. She didn't know that most men would consider themselves fortunate if she deigned to smile in their direction.

In his past, Ben had known his share of glamorous women. He'd even been propositioned by a few. At the time, he'd been indifferent to their attention; he had been devoted to Jeanette, his wife. Like a fool, he'd remained faithful to her, which Jeanette, he was later to learn, had not. Yet even now, even after the heartache of Jeanette's disloyalty, Ben Eaton was still a one-woman-at-a-time kind of man. Intuitively, he sensed that Rachel Daniels was a one-man-at-a-time kind of woman. Funny that they should be so opposite and yet so similar.

She set the toddy before him, smiling in the disarming way he'd come to appreciate. She said nothing for a moment, which made him wonder what she was thinking. "Have you anything other than bluejeans to wear tomorrow?" she asked.

"I'll be presentable" was all he said.

She studied him as she blew on her Irish coffee. "You're divorced, aren't you, Ben?"

He had not anticipated the question, and it showed. He took a swig of the toddy before answering, "Yes."

"Has your ex-wife something to do with your dislike of Dallas?"

Again, he was surprised by her query. "Partially."

"If you'd prefer not to discuss it, I'll understand. God knows I can appreciate reluctance to admit an unsatisfactory marriage." She took a hefty swig of the toddy herself. "If my husband hadn't died prematurely, I'm fairly certain our marriage would have suffered a similar outcome."

That casually spoken commentary about her own marriage truly stunned Ben. Oh, sure, he hadn't forgotten Bubba's intimation to the contrary, but never had Miz Daniels uttered a derogatory word about her late husband until now. It was his turn to question her. "I was under the impression that you were happily married."

"At the time of Yancy's death, our marriage was in about the same state of decline as this farm. All my husband left me with was a precious daughter, a few good memories, and troubles galore. Yancy hadn't the disposition for farming." A sad smile graced her lips. "Actually, his maverick nature would have been better suited to a less restrictive life-style. The isolation out here made him antsy, and he got no satisfaction from reaping a harvest. Looking back, I now realize how mismatched we really were. I'm sure he must've often wished for a more carefree wife, just as I often longed for a more dependable husband."

Once again, Ben recalled the gossip that Bubba had volunteered during the ride from Lubbock. The alleged liaison between Rachel's late husband and the icehouse barmaid fit the usual pattern of the restless-husband syndrome. Although he doubted that Rachel would be surprised to learn of her husband's infidelity, he hoped she would be spared the knowledge. He knew from personal experience how embittering the truth of a spouse's betrayal can be. No matter what one's suspicions are, confirmation of an adulterous act is as traumatic after the fact as it is at the time, maybe even more so because of the "being the last to know" connotation.

He wished Bubba hadn't told him about Yancy's extramarital activities. Somehow, it made him feel like an accomplice. It was absurd, he knew. Yet Rachel was such a forthright person that even such a minor concealment on his part bothered him. He glanced away, seizing on an ominous rumble in the heavens as an excuse. "Sounds like it might rain."

His sudden change of subject took her off guard. "I take it you'd prefer not to discuss either of our former marriages." She collected his empty cup, then made a move to rise from her chair. A touch of his hand delayed her retreat.

"It's not that I'm being deliberately evasive, Rachel," he explained. "My ex-wife is part of a past I'd just as soon forget. Suffice it to say that my life was very different then. You'd probaby be amazed at the hundred-and-eighty-degree turn it has taken since Dallas and Jeanette. I'm not the same man that I was three years ago. Funny" —he grinned the sort of grin that implies a private joke— "I once thought of my ordeal as a curse. Now I'm not so sure it wasn't a blessing."

Unwillingly, her eyes drifted to the tanned hand that still sheathed hers. Involuntarily, she found herself comparing manly touches. Yancy's had been stirring and flighty; Ben's was steadfast and compelling. "It's hard to begin again, especially when you have to do it alone. I don't think anyone comes through such an experience without battle scars."

He nodded, withdrawing his hand and easing back into the chair with a pensive look. "Your scars don't show, Rachel." His hazel eyes traveled over her appreciatively.

47

In spite of herself, she felt a flush coming on. Quickly, she stood and made an unnecessary fuss rinsing the toddy mugs. "It's made me hard on the inside. I don't intend ever to relinquish control of my life to someone else again. Yancy insisted on having sole say over every matter, big or small. And you see the result." She slapped a dish towel over her shoulder disgustedly. "Never will I again entrust mine and Meggie's future into a man's hands. The only reason I did so with Yancy was because disagreeing with his decisions, good or bad as they might have been, was an insult to his manly pride. If I hadn't been so damned concerned about his ego and had been more aware of our shaky situation, I wouldn't be in this stalemated mess." Her gaze was fixed beyond the kitchen window, as if she were trying to envision a future free of the past mistakes and their present repercussions. "I get so angry when I think about how Yancy left us. Sometimes I think he crashed into that tractor trailer on purpose rather than face the consequences of his irresponsibility." After voicing aloud the secret grudge she bore her dead husband, the widow spun around and cast her hired hand a retracting look.

"That's a natural thought to harbor," he assured her.

"Probably," she agreed, although her tone was none too positive. "How about you, Ben? What hidden scars or secret grudges do you hold?"

He was tempted to confide in her—sorely tempted—but that manly pride to which she'd earlier referred curbed the impulse. "I've had more time than you to lick my wounds and distance myself from the past" was all he said.

Rachel admired his understated style, although she questioned whether he had made a total break with the past. Something told her it haunted him even yet. He was gazing at her in that disturbing way of his, as if she were dressed in tissue paper and he could see every minute detail of her body. She fiddled with the towel, neatly folding it and draping it over the sink. Then she glanced at the clock on the wall. "Goodness, I didn't realize it was so late. It'd be a shame if I were to oversleep the one time you decided to put in an appearance at the Sunday services."

He got up from the wooden chair and stretched in that lazy way to which she'd become accustomed. "A shame," he repeated, a wry smile breaking on his sun-baked lips.

"As much as I'd like to believe those grumbles in the heavens mean rain, they could as well be a sign from the Almighty. I surely hope that lightning won't strike us tomorrow, Mr. Eaton. Meggie and I are taking a big chance, sitting in the same pew with such a sinner." Her dimples magically appeared as she sashayed past him. "Remember to switch off the light before you turn in, will you, please? 'Night, Ben," she called to him, and then her willowy figure disappeared up the staircase.

He shook his head bemusedly, muttering to himself, "Yeah, sleep well, Rachel. At least one of us shouldn't be deprived of sweet dreams."

With a disapproving cluck, Meggie flipped the pages of the hymnal she and Ben were sharing to the correct song. She was playing the role of a harried guardian angel to the hilt and was loving every minute of it.

From the corner of her eye, Rachel caught her daughter's slight scoot closer toward Ben and smothered a smile. Ever since breakfast Meggie had been mothering him through the Sunday penance, and, judging from her smug expression, the imp was quite pleased with herself at her accomplishment. At the concluding chorus of

"Amen," Rachel closed her own hymnal and stole a glimpse at her hired hand as Pastor Loggins assumed the pulpit.

Ben certainly did look nice—even better than the "presentable" that he'd promised. In fact, attired as he was in a navy pinstripe suit, a white shirt with monogrammed cuffs, and a burgundy silk tie, he was the best-dressed man in the whole of the congregation. The man wore a suit well, as if he were accustomed to such finery and it were second nature to him to be the focus of attention. And his outfit wasn't bargain store, either. It was plain that his ensemble was first class, not secondhand. The initials on the cuffs were his own—B.E.E. She found herself wondering what the middle initial stood for and why an aimless drifter would possess such fine clothes. And she wasn't the only one who found his appearance provocative. Except for Annie Baird, who was ninety-two and blind, the godfearing folk of Mesquite Junction had collectively taken account of the stranger in their midst, especially Desiree Sayer, who all but gawked during the invocation. Rachel could only imagine *her* thoughts. She was probably scheming how to wheedle an introduction. Flirtation, not salvation, was most assuredly on Desiree's mind.

"We all stray from time to time," Pastor Loggins was reminding the congregation. "We all have moments of weakness when unpure thoughts and unchristian attitudes seize us." Rachel sat straighter in the pew, afraid the good reverend could read her mind and her heart. She tried to concentrate on the sermon's message rather than on Desiree Sayer's questionable morals and on her preoccupation with Ben Eaton. It was hard, though, especially when Desiree kept looking over and licking her lips like some Persian cat anticipating cream. Geez, but she was obvious—no modesty whatsoever.

"We must be strong and reject the devil's influence. The strength you seek is in Scripture, brothers and sisters. The strength to deny Satan . . . to deny those sinful impulses of lust and greed that lure you from grace." Pastor Loggins's sermon was particularly fervent this Sunday—particularly damning to Rachel. God only knew how many times in the past month she'd entertained notions of lust. She lowered her eyes, idly rearranging the hem of her skirt.

". . . And to those of you who *have* strayed from the fold, who've been lured by an untrue light and lost your way, I invite you to rejoin the flock, to reaffirm your faith. Come forth today. For tomorrow it may be too late," Pastor Loggins implored.

Ben sat stonefaced, ignoring Meggie's urgent nudges. Good grief! What was he doing in this country church, singing "Amazing Grace" and enduring yet another windy sermon? He felt like a colossal hypocrite. As much as he'd like to dispel Meggie's fear about his eternal damnation, he had no intention of joining the procession of lost souls marching up the aisle to redeem themselves. Long ago he'd made a pact with the Almighty: he wouldn't bother God with any more petitions if God wouldn't bother him with any more claims on his disillusioned soul. He believed in hell. He'd personally gone through it a few years back. But heaven? Well, that was another matter entirely.

Meggie inspected her lace-trimmed anklets and shiny black patent shoes primly. She was disappointed that Ben refused to be saved, but she was certainly not discouraged. The words *it cannot be done* were simply not in her vocabulary. Before the dismissal hymn was over, she was already thinking ahead to next Sunday and how best to get Ben to visit God's house again.

She tucked her hand into his as they rose from the pew. "See, that wasn't so bad," she cajoled as they weaved through the throng of worshipers.

Once outside, he drew a cathartic breath before venturing a tight smile. "We must've gotten separated from your mother. Do you see her, Meggie?"

The tyke shaded her eyes and scanned the crowd of familiar faces until she spotted her mother near the church doors. "She's over there, talking to Mr. McMurtry." Ben followed the point of her finger, noting that Rachel was engaged in conversation with a gentleman who looked more cosmopolitan than rural. Ben's green eyes narrowed as he asked, "Who's Mr. McMurtry?"

"Mama's old beau," Meggie stated matter-of-factly. "Daddy used to get mad, real mad, whenever Mr. McMurtry talked to Mama after church. He used to say that Mr. McMurtry only came to Sunday service so he could show off in front of her."

Ben's curiosity—the only rational label he could come up with for the inexplicable feeling he was experiencing—was aroused. "What does Mr. McMurtry do around here?"

"I dunno," Meggie replied disinterestedly, since her attention had been diverted by the approach of Desiree Sayer. She tried to warn Ben about the afflicted divorcee, but it was too late. Like a swarm of honeybees, Desiree was upon them.

"Warm, isn't it?" the divorcee drawled, fanning herself with her wide-brimmed hat.

Ben smiled politely, pretending not to notice the clinch of Meggie's tiny hand. "Yes, ma'am, it is," he said pleasantly.

"You must be the new hand over at the Daniels place," she concluded with a saucy flip of her ebony hair. "I'm Desiree Sayer, a friend and neighbor of Rachel's." The brunette followed up the introduction with a sultry smile.

"Ben Eaton," he supplied, taking inventory of the woman and making a quick assessment of her. He'd met women like her before—artificially pretty and conveniently available.

"An interesting name," she said. "I make a study of people's names. Sometimes they fit a person, and sometimes they don't. I suspect yours suits you just fine. Like I said, interesting." She slanted him a coy look before acknowledging Meggie. "You're looking sweet as ever, Margaret Jane. Tell your mama I said hello, won't you?"

Meggie gave her a wary nod, then eyed the ground.

Desiree replaced her hat atop her head and flashed Ben a parting smile. "It's a small town, Ben Eaton. I'm sure we'll be bumping into each other from time to time."

"Probably" was all he said as she took her leave.

"Whew!" Meggie exhaled a relieved sigh.

Ben stared at the child, perplexed by her attitude. "Would you like to explain why you were squeezing my hand at Miz Sayer's every word?" he inquired.

"You shouldn't be talking to her, Ben. She's a nymphowhack," she explained.

"A what?"

"A nymphowhack," she repeated. "But don't worry. She didn't touch you or anything, so I don't think you can catch it."

Ben had difficulty deciphering Meggie's meaning. "What exactly is a nymphowhack?"

"Someone who's got sex and can give it to you," she elaborated.

"Oh," he said, trying to maintain his composure. "And

how is it that you know about her—ailment?" He tried to phrase Miz Sayer's malady as delicately as possible.

"Mama said she was a nymphowhack. I wasn't sure what that was, so I asked my friend Dory Phillips. She looked it up in the dictionary and told me. I thought I ought to warn you. But it's okay, I think, 'cause you didn't touch her or anything like that." She paused, then added knowingly, "Just don't get too close. Okay?"

He nearly choked but managed a nod.

"I'm sorry you had to wait." Rachel rescued Ben before he succumbed to the pent-up laughter threatening to explode.

"Miz Sayer was talking to Ben," Meggie blurted. "He won't catch her nymphowhack, will he, Mama?"

Rachel immediately knew of what her daughter spoke. Instantly, a crimson blush suffused her cheeks. She couldn't meet Ben's eyes as she caught Meggie's hand and began to march toward the car.

"Will he, Mama?" Meggie badgered.

"Wherever did you get such an idea?" Rachel sputtered before thinking.

"From you" was the honest reply. "You fussed at Daddy for drinking cider with her at the bazaar. You said she was a nymphowhack. Remember?"

"Not now, Margaret Jane. We can discuss this in private later." Rachel opened the car door, her expression unmistakably annoyed.

Meggie wisely deduced that it was in her own best interest to abide by her mother's wishes. "Yes, ma'am," she agreed, climbing into the back seat.

Ben decided it was in *his* own best interest not to pursue the subject. The threesome drove home in silence. It wasn't until Meggie was otherwise occupied upstairs that Rachel dared to broach the subject of Desiree Sayer.

54

Ben happened to be pouring himself a glass of cider at the time.

"The correct term for Desiree Sayer is nymphomaniac," she informed him. "And if I were you, I'd stay clear of the woman. I'm sure she can be most generous with certain favors, but not without a purpose. She always expects something in return."

Ben loosened his tie, then challenged her righteous posture with a cavalier grin. "Most women usually do want something in return. Some are just more discreet, is all."

She visibly bristled but did not rebut the cynical observation. "Dinner is in one hour" was all she said before storming from the kitchen.

"I can't wait." His sarcastic mutter went unheard. When it came to mealtime around the farm, Ben expected the worst and was usually not disappointed. What Rachel chose to serve usually came frozen or in a can.

Finishing off the cider, he stepped out onto the back porch to clear his head of the widow's provocative perfume. Desiree Sayer had been right about it being unusually warm, he thought to himself while looking out over the blossoming fields. He'd often noted that tensions ran high when the temperature climbed. Although the prevailing mood in Mesquite Junction seemed serene and the cotton crop appeared to be thriving, he had a strong premonition that the hot, arid weather wouldn't be the only variable this season. Yes, indeed. A strong premonition.

CHAPTER FOUR

Rachel knew her daughter well. Just as she'd predicted, Meggie was not appeased by Ben's one pilgrimage to the country church. Every Sunday thereafter, Margaret Jane found yet another compelling reason for Ben to attend the services. This Sunday, she wheedled and wrangled his attendance with the annual Box Supper Auction.

"It's real special, Ben," the little minx coaxed. "Mama's box supper is gonna be raffled, and you just gotta bid. It wouldn't look right if you didn't. People might think you don't like her cookin'. You don't want to shame her, do you?"

Although Ben was hardly inclined to endorse Rachel's culinary ability, he could not in good conscience publicly embarrass her by declining either to attend the affair or to bid on her box supper, especially since Meggie attached such significance to the event. Impatiently, Meggie tugged on his pants leg, demanding, "Well, are you or aren't you gonna do it?"

In the middle of replacing another worn belt on the overworked tractor and not much in the mood to be harassed, Ben agreed with only a minimal protest. "I'm sure your mother won't lack for bids, but I guess a little added insurance wouldn't hurt."

Quite pleased with herself at having persuaded Ben to

attend the charitable affair, Meggie fairly beamed. "Betcha Mama's box supper fetches the best offer of all. Whoever bids the highest gets to share it with her." She bent to inspect a glittering object half-buried in the dirt. "My friend Dory says that sometimes the men get more than just a picnic supper for their money," she prattled while digging in the chalky soil to retrieve a grimy dime.

Ben continued to tinker with the tractor's belt. "Is that so?" he said distractedly.

"Yup." She spat on the dime and wiped it on the front of her Care Bear–decaled T-shirt. "Sometimes they get a big old smooch."

The taut belt snapped free of his grip at the unexpected remark. He turned and cast Meggie a quizzical glance. "A smooch?" he repeated.

Engrossed in buffing her treasure to a dazzling sheen, Meggie nodded affirmatively. "That's when grownups close their eyes and touch lips—like this." She demonstrated a pucker. "A smooch is different than a plain kiss. It's more gushy and real yucky," she explained, examining her shiny bounty for defects. "I think it probably hurts your mouth, too, 'cause grownups always moan like they got a tummyache when they do it. What I can't figure out is why anybody would want to smooch. It's as dumb as eating green apples when you know for sure they're gonna give you the cramps." Inquisitiveness gleamed in her brown eyes as she lifted her gaze to his. "You ever smooched, Ben?"

He decided to be reservedly candid. "Once or twice."

"Did it make you sick?"

"Not that I recall."

"Mmm," she mulled. That's probably 'cause you got a strong constitution. That means you don't get sick easy."

Ben shook his head amusedly. "I suppose that's another revelation, courtesy of Dory Phillips and her trusty dictionary."

"Naw," Meggie drawled. "That's what Mama said about me the time Cory Thompson and I had a dare about who could drink the most witches' brew. We made it ourselves out of raspberry Kool-Aid, pickle juice, lemon peel, hot pepper, chocolate syrup, and the dab of beer left in the bottom of a case of empties his Daddy stored on the back porch. Cory upchucked and couldn't go to school for two days. I won the dare and was just fine."

Ben was duly impressed. "I'd say that definitely takes a strong constitution, all right. Remind me never to challenge you to a chugging contest."

Meggie gnawed her bottom lip thoughtfully, then grasped Ben's hand and placed the polished dime into his palm. "Here, I want you to take this and use it to bid on Mama's box supper. Since you got a strong constitution, too, I want to make sure that if she smooches with anybody, it'll be with you. Maybe it'll rub off and Mama won't get sick neither." With an infectious giggle, she hightailed it across the yard.

Ben stared at the silver object, his heart full of Meggie and his stomach churning at the thought of consuming Rachel's repugnant box supper. A rueful smirk flitted over his lips—he couldn't recall a single instance when those whom he'd loved in his past had even pretended to make such a concession on his behalf. He flipped the dime into the air, recaptured it, and tucked it into his hip pocket for safekeeping. Never would he relinquish the symbolic dime, for it represented something much more precious than its actual worth, something he had almost believed was passé—unconditional love.

* * *

Since the annual Box Supper Auction was one of six celebrated occasions in the small community—the others being Christmas, Easter, Thanksgiving, Independence Day, and the Harvest Social—nearly all of Mesquite Junction was on hand. Even those scarlet individuals whose Christian attitudes were questionable elected to attend and were generally welcomed today.

Everyone was decked in their summer finest. The ladies wore pastels and smelled of sweet talc, and the gents were clean-shaven and sported spit-shined shoes rather than work-scarred boots. Rachel and Ben looked as elegant as the others—she wore a polished cotton, striped wraparound dress of pale mauve and green, and he had donned white pleated slacks and an open-neck polo shirt. Not too many of those present recognized the prestigious insignia displayed on the shirt's pocket, but Rachel noted it and secretly wondered once again about Ben's trendy attire. Where and how had a drifter acquired such style?

The church hall was draped in sunny crepe-paper streamers, and the wooden auctioneer platform was an explosion of yellow and white polka-dot balloons. There were row upon row of neatly placed folding chairs, and an endless string of tables displaying various homemade foodstuffs and crafts lined the perimeter of the spacious hall. The townsfolk milled about, browsing the wares, sampling the delectable goodies, and chatting cordially with their neighbors. The excited murmur of adult chatter was interspersed with an occasional shriek of delight from the playful children.

But the sight, smell, and sound that captured Ben's attention immediately upon entering the buzzing hall was the snack booth in a far corner, where one might purchase a sausage on a stick or a wedge of pecan pie for a minimal fee. He cast a dubious look at the picnic basket dangling from Rachel's hand and breathed a silent sigh of relief. Considering his meager finances, he doubted he'd outdo the other bidders, but in the event that her culinary reputation preceded her and he was forced to champion her honor, he'd at least be able to get some backup nourishment.

"Isn't this fun, Ben? Look over yonder! There's a peashoot booth where you can win prizes. Last year, Dory Phillips's dad won a giant stuffed teddy bear for her." Antsy with anticipation, Meggie shifted her weight from foot to foot. "I'll bet you can best Mr. Phillips this year, Ben. Can we try?"

Rachel placed a calming hand on her daughter's shoulder. "We've just arrived, and already you're pestering, honey. Give Ben a while to get his bearings."

"We'll take a shot at that teddy bear a little later," Ben promised with a wink.

A "yo, Meggie!" beckoned the tyke from across the hall. "Okay," she relented, glancing at her mother for permission to run free with her friends.

"Don't get into any mischief, Margaret Jane. And do try to remember that young ladies do not turn somersaults or swing by their knees when wearing a dress."

"Yes, ma'am" was the sheepish reply before the tot skipped off to join her playmates.

"I hope Meggie minds my instructions this year." Watching her daughter scamper through the crowd, Rachel unintentionally voiced a private concern aloud. "At the last box supper, some of the older boys dared her to hang by her knees from the top bar of the Jungle Jim out back, just so they could get a peek at her flowered underwear and tease her unmercifully for weeks."

Ben did not find the incident especially unusual or

traumatic. "I wouldn't concern myself too much. Peeking and teasing is just part of the natural process of growing up."

Rachel lost sight of her daughter when the pack of children dashed out the doors. She turned to Ben with a frown. "Meggie is a born tomboy. When the boys made fun of her sissy panties, she insisted that I buy her jockey underwear and threatened to go in the raw every chance she got if I didn't abide by her wishes. It took many a lengthy and persuasive discussion between the two of us before I convinced her otherwise."

In spite of Rachel's legitimate vexation, Ben had to laugh.

"It wasn't funny at the time," Rachel insisted, although a grudging chuckle broke from her, too. "Sometimes Meggie is almost more than a person can handle."

"I'm sure she is," he conceded. "But her independent spirit is what makes her so special. Try to channel it, but never, ever smother it in her, Rachel. In the end, a person's character is all one truly has. Everything else is irrelevant."

Their eyes met and held for a moment. She tried to decipher the intensity she detected, and he admired the sensitivity he beheld.

"Afternoon, Rachel." Bubba Atkins interrupted the silent exchange. "You're looking mighty good. Have ya got some of that tasty fried chicken of yours in that basket? Surely would like to bid on it myself, but the missus would be highly upset. She gave me strict orders that I have to hike up the bidding for Jo Mae. She's got some funny notion that our daughter will wind up an old maid at twenty if we don't help the cause along." The friendly neighbor had a reputation for being a nonstop talker, which his windy greeting verified. "Well, well, if it ain't the hitchhiker himself. How've you been?" He gave Ben's hand a hearty shake. "It appears I was wrong. Rachel must've needed help worse than I thought. Circumstances being what they are, she wouldn't squander good money unless it was essential."

Rachel visibly stiffened at Atkins's insinuation about her situation and finances. What's more, Bubba had inadvertently revealed the fact that it was he who had recommended to Ben that he seek out her farm. Why had Ben pretended not to remember the meddling old gent's identity? She wondered what else he kept to himself. "Mr. Eaton is only working for me temporarily," she said defensively. "After the harvest, I should be in a position to handle things quite capably alone."

"Now, don't go gettin' your dander up, Rachel. It ain't no sin to admit that a woman can't run a farm by her lonesome. Some of us tried to warn ya that it'd be rough going," he reminded her.

"And I told you then, just like I'm telling you now—I can manage just fine without a man."

Her bobbed nose lifted only a millimeter, but it was enough that Ben could perceive the affront to her pride. "I heard a rumor that one of your neighbors is in a worse bind than Miz Daniels," he said. "A fellow by the name of Jake Simmons. I suppose it doesn't matter much whether you're male or female when the odds are against a farm making it through another year. Times are hard, and some good *men* are going under." He made his point so subtly that Bubba never realized he'd been soundly refuted.

Rachel caught Ben's intent and was grateful for his unsolicited loyalty. "If you gentlemen will excuse me, I really should see about placing my supper up for auction.

If you're still interested in those adjoining acres, come by sometime, and we'll discuss price, Bubba."

"Shoot, Rachel. The only way I could take those acres off your hands is if ya was giving 'em away. The missus won't let me touch our savings. Says it's only to be used to give Jo Mae a proper wedding. Hell, slow as that girl is to hook a man, I'll probably be dead and buried long before the ceremony. I may drop by for a cup of coffee and a piece of your fine apple pie, though."

Ben couldn't believe his ears. Was Bubba serious? To the extent of his knowledge, Rachel Daniels could hardly boil water, let alone bake a fine apple pie. Something was wrong. Either Bubba Atkins was being unbelievably gracious, or the widow had been reneging on meals. His suspicion aroused, he cast the widow a probing look.

"You're welcome to stop by whenever the mood moves you, Bubba. Have a nice day," she bade the neighbor, then flashed Ben a startlingly warm smile and walked off. It made him all the more leery. Could the woman actually cook as well as Bubba had implied? Then why in the hell was she holding out on him? Sheer damned stubbornness, he was sure. The thought made him mulishly determined to sample the widow's box supper so that he could justly accuse her of malicious malnourishment.

"That's one headstrong woman." Bubba removed his straw hat and raked his stubby fingers through his hair. "Ain't no way she's gonna fare any better than poor Jake Simmons. She shoulda sold out for what she could get when she had the chance. There's rumors that Jake will be auctioned off before the end of the season, and I'd lay money on the fact that Rachel's farm will be the next to go."

"How much would you be willing to wager?" Ben's

voice was so cool and deliberate, it sent a twinge of wariness through Bubba.

"I'm fond of Rachel," the old man was quick to say. "Hope to goodness she proves me wrong and hangs on. We folk don't like to see none of our neighbors go under, 'cause we know that, except for the grace of God, it coulda been any one of us. It's like a death in the family when a farm is auctioned. We all mourn." He hung his head respectfully and muttered, "Nope. Couldn't wager on such a thing as Rachel losing her place. Wouldn't be fittin'." He raised his eyes, making contact with Ben's and issuing an unmistakable dare. "But I wouldn't be opposed to a small wager on the rain we're needing so badly." A lazy grin broke upon his face. "I'll betcha a hundred dollars we get us a soaker afore mid-August."

"If you win, you'll have to wait until harvest time to collect." Ben made no bones about his financial state. Neither did he offer any excuse or apology.

"That's okay. I can smell rain when it's weeks off," Bubba bragged. "I'm so sure, I'll pay up in mid-August if I'm wrong."

"Whatever you want," Ben agreed as they shook hands on the wager.

"Funny, but somehow I didn't figure ya to be a gambling man," the old man noted, scratching his neck at the point where his stiff collar met his protruding Adam's apple.

"I'm not usually. I just know it isn't going to rain before early September. I also know that Rachel Daniels's farm won't end up on any auction block" was Ben's confident comeback. *Not if I can help it,* he silently vowed to himself, refusing to accept Bubba's forecast of doom.

"Psychic, are ya?" Bubba half grunted, half laughed.

"No. I just can't smell either rain or foreclosure in the air." Ben glanced around, giving the appearance of having dismissed the bet from his mind.

"Well, tell ya what I think—" Bubba drawled thoughtfully.

Ben would've preferred that he keep his thoughts to himself, but he knew that was unlikely. The old man's grin became wily, and Ben instantly became uneasy.

"—I think you're kinda fond of Rachel yourself. Yessiree! I think you got more than just a hired hand's passing interest in that farm's future. And I figure that's an okay thing since Rachel needs a man around the place. A little sowing and reaping in the biblical sense ain't gonna hurt her none either, if ya catch my drift." A nudge of his elbow into Ben's ribs clearly defined his meaning.

"I hope you're better at smelling rain than you are at subtlety. If not, you're gonna be a hundred dollars poorer come mid-August. See you around, Bubba."

Before Bubba could blink or mumble "Yeah, good talking with ya," Ben had taken his leave and was walking off in the direction of the pea-shoot booth to take some practice shots.

The coveted teddy bear clutched under her arm, Meggie stood beside "the greatest pea shooter in the county" with her hand possessively tucked in his and awaited the upcoming raffle of her mother's supper. She looked over her shoulder and stuck out her tongue at the pouting Dory Phillips. Since Dory was such a sore loser, Meggie did not feel the least bit guilty about lording it over her friend.

She did, however, suffer a smidgeon of conscience because of the braggadocious fib she'd told her playmates when they'd asked her about Ben's background. Well, so what if she'd awed them with that wild tale of Ben being a former grand champion bull-rider on the rodeo circuit whose glory days had ended when he was gored in an unmentionable place by a raging, fire-snorting bull? She'd had her fingers crossed behind her back the whole time she had wowed 'em with the story. Besides, it served 'em right! They were always bragging about their fathers' feats, and time and again they had made her feel envious because she didn't have any such awesome accounts to relate. Just this once, *she* was the center of attention, and the little white lie that made her chums bug-eyed with hero worship just made it that much sweeter. Triumphantly, she looked away from Dory and waited for the bidding on her mother's picnic basket to begin.

"The next basket to be auctioned belongs to Rachel Daniels," the blustery auctioneer announced. "Now, gents, I expect to hear some powerful bidding, since it's a well-established fact that Rachel's fried chicken can make a body's mouth water at the mere mention of it. Bidding will commence at a minimum of ten dollars. Who'll give me ten?"

Meggie urged Ben to open, but before he could comply, Jonas McMurtry, Rachel's onetime beau, spoke up. "Fifteen dollars," he said assertively.

A squeeze of Ben's hand by the determined Meggie made him counter with a bid of twenty dollars.

"I have twenty. Do I hear twenty-five?" the auctioneer asked.

A resounding "Thirty" boomed from Jonas as he straightened in his chair and took note of the outsider who was standing apart and holding the hand of Rachel's child.

"Offer more, Ben," Meggie insisted under her breath. Ben was fast reaching the end of his limited funds. After slanting a look in McMurtry's direction and analyzing his intractable profile, he knew it was futile to continue bidding. Nonetheless, he offered a thirty-five-dollar bid for Meggie's sake. Damn! He'd really wanted to taste that fried chicken to see if there was indeed some truth to Rachel's reputation as a cook. Her old beau was becoming a nuisance. Maybe Rachel's late husband had had good reason to dislike the pompous ass. Ben didn't much care for him—not with his dandylike looks and the superior manner with which he seemed to regard everyone else.

The good folk of Mesquite Junction sensed the rivalry between the two men. Like sports fans at Wimbledon watching a major match, their heads swiveled in unison as each opponent made a bid.

"I have a thirty-five-dollar bid from the gent in the far corner. Am I offered more?" The auctioneer's yodel grew more zealous.

Jonas McMurtry's blue eyes traveled from Rachel's flushed face to the cool-looking hired hand, sizing up his competition. "Forty," he bid. A collective twitter of excitement rippled over the onlookers. Almost everyone present knew that McMurtry and Rachel had been an item a long time ago. It was also common knowledge that ever since Jonas's divorce several years before and Yancy's recent passing, his interest in the widow had been rekindled. McMurtry's motives they understood, but it was the interloper's interest that fueled public speculation. Forty dollars was an exorbitantly high sum to pay for the privilege of sharing a box supper with Rachel, no matter how good her chicken might be.

Rachel couldn't believe what was happening. Nor could she decide whether to be flattered or embarrassed. She knew very well that the town gossips would have a field day tomorrow recounting the incident. Jonas was behaving as if he had an undisputed right to her fried chicken, and Ben was bidding as if the contents of her basket were vital to his well-being. Why would he do such a thing? she wondered. Surely it wasn't that he craved her company. She would've thought he'd welcome a break from her.

Rachel caught a glimpse of Desiree Sayer's face. Judging from the divorcee's piqued expression, she was not at all pleased with the attention the bid was drawing, especially from Ben. Rachel couldn't resist the temptation to gloat a little—silently, of course. Secretly, though, she was skeptical of Ben's motives. Was this Meggie's doing? It had all the markings. Or perhaps Mr. Eaton just wished to satisfy his chauvinistic curiosity about her cooking. If that were the case, it would serve him right to have to pay a ransom for the privilege.

"Forty is the bid. Do I hear another?" The auctioneer looked directly at Ben.

Meggie held her breath. Ben couldn't afford to raise the bid, but McMurtry's smug grin and some devilish impulse made him hike it anyway. He gambled that the cocky fool would pay any price to save face. At first, Ben hadn't liked him on general principle. Now it was becoming personal. "I'll double the last bid," he declared loud and clear. The teddy bear bounced up and down with Meggie's gleeful jumps. An audible gasp traveled over the townsfolk, and most of them missed McMurtry's visible wince. But Ben noted the slight admission, and he knew his initial opinion of McMurtry was correct. The man was superficial, and Rachel had better beware.

Jonas had no choice. He was not to be outdone by a nobody in front of Rachel and the whole darned town. After all, he had an esteemed economic position in the

68

county to uphold. If he were to back down now, it might set a precedent. Everyone would think they could haggle over the price of seeds and supplies—*his* price—and this he would not tolerate.

"One hundred dollars," he offered, at which point Rachel blanched.

The auctioneer was as astonished as everyone else in the hall. He faltered when he reaffirmed the bid. "I, ah, I have a hundred dollars from Mr. McMurtry. Is there a counterbid?"

Dead silence.

Everyone looked at Ben as the auctioneer raised his gavel. "Goin' once" was heard. Meggie's heart sank to her shoes as Ben stood mute. "Goin' twice," the auctioneer chanted. Ben contemplated bidding, but good sense won out, and he refrained. Rachel's heart rate accelerated as she awaited the final outcome. "Sold to Jonas McMurtry for one hundred dollars," the auctioneer bellowed, slamming the gavel down on the podium and settling the matter as neighbor turned to neighbor to confer about what they'd just witnessed.

"That darned well better be the finest batch of chicken you ever whooped up, Rachel." The auctioneer tried to ease the tension with levity. "Come on up here, Jonas, and claim your basket," he invited, then got ready to auction the next box supper on the agenda.

McMurtry stood and glared at his rival through the thicket of folk who were offering their respectful—if disbelieving—congratulations. Intuitively, he sensed that the hired hand had manipulated him. But why? he wondered. Was it possible that the lowly field hand thought of himself as a contender for Rachel's attentions? The idea was preposterous as far as he was concerned. He'd waited a long time to reinsert himself into Rachel's life, and he wasn't about to let some nobody drifter outshine him in her eyes. Eaton was the man's name, a meddling busybody had whispered while patting him on the back, Ben Eaton. McMurtry wouldn't forget that name, anymore than he would dismiss the deliberate affront or the man's living under Rachel's roof. Jonas squared his shoulders and leveled Ben a final spurning glance. Then he settled his bid and possessively escorted Rachel to a secluded picnic table outside the hall.

At the doorway, her steps lagged and she turned to survey the chaos in the wake of the excessive bidding. Ben was trying to console the foot-stomping Meggie. So it was as she had thought. Obviously, her daughter had designed the whole scheme to guarantee her mother a suitable companion for the evening. The little conniver! She was truly becoming much too big for her britches.

When she felt the press of Jonas's hand on her back, she remembered herself and the dear price he'd paid for the honor of sharing her supper. She smiled cordially up at him as he swung wide the door, but her thoughts were still on Ben Eaton. She had a strange yearning to be with him, if only for an isolated hour, under circumstances where she was not the hard boss-woman and he was not the deferring hired hand, when they could be two equal individuals with a chance to meet on equal ground. Regardless of Meggie's interference, she would've liked to sit with Ben and learn a little more about the enigmatic stranger who'd happened into her life. As much as she hated to admit it, his attentiveness had been flattering. In fact, in his own understated way, Ben Eaton was becoming more and more appealing to her. A chemistry was at work between them.

She stepped through the door and welcomed the summer breeze. It cleared her head of the unthinkable notion that she might succumb to the charms of a drifter. No way! She'd once cared for Jonas McMurtry enough to consider surrendering her virginity to him before marriage. But even he had been unable to pierce her prudent defenses. So Ben Eaton surely could not tempt her to compromise her morals now, no matter how appealing he might be!

By the time the picnic was over, Meggie was miserable and blatantly sulking. As it turned out, not only had Rachel foiled her plans by sharing her box supper and exclusive company with Jonas McMurtry, but Ben had become the sole bidder for Desiree Sayer's basket, since no other man had the courage to incur his mate's wrath by acknowledging the town harlot. Although Ben had explained to Meggie that he'd felt obliged to make a token offer in order to salvage the shunned divorcee's wounded pride, Meggie had not been convinced. To her mind, it would serve Ben and her mama right if they both got the cramping miseries from smooching with Mr. McMurtry and Miz Sayer. And she was pretty certain they had smooched, 'cause both of 'em were looking awfully sour and not conversing a'tall.

"You've been noticeably quiet all the way home, Meggie. Is something bothering you?" Rachel spoke in a restrained, monotone voice, which was her habit when annoyed, as she set the empty basket on the kitchen table.

Meggie hugged her teddy bear closer and hung her head dejectedly. "I just wanted Ben to win the bidding so you, me, and him could share your box supper together, is all," she confessed.

"I thought as much." Rachel brushed past Ben as if he were invisible and assumed a predisciplinary stance in front of her daughter. Tipping her chin with a fingertip,

71

she forced the tot to gaze up into her solemn eyes. "You'll learn, Margaret Jane, that whenever you tamper with the natural course of things, it can backfire on you. I strongly suspect that you had no small hand in that showy bidding. It was an improper and immodest display, and I'm very displeased with you."

"Yes, ma'am," Meggie uttered contritely, twiddling with the teddy bear's black button nose.

"Well, what's done is done." Rachel's frosty tone thawed a bit, but she did not totally relent. "I think you should go on up to bed now. Perhaps after you've slept on this, you'll see the wrong in tampering."

Meggie looked helplessly at Ben, who was remaining neutral during this private matter between mother and daughter. "What are you going to call your bear?" he asked soothingly.

"Benny," she answered, at which his heartstrings gave a tug.

He winked at her. " 'Night, honey."

"Yeah, 'night, Ben," she replied, the teddy bear dangling from her small hand as she retreated toward her room.

"I'll be up in a moment to tuck you in," Rachel offered, wishing she could retract the punishment but knowing that Meggie must be disciplined occasionally, regardless of how hard it was on them both.

Meggie paused and turned to her mother, her brows knit in quandary. "How come whenever grownups displease, they don't have to go to bed early and think on it?"

Ben had to turn his back quickly and pretend to be engrossed in an unopened newspaper on the kitchen counter. The question Meggie posed was a valid one.

"They may not have to go to bed early, but they do

72

think on it, Margaret Jane. Believe me they do," Rachel explained.

Meggie shrugged, then dragged herself and the newly christened Benny off to bed.

Once the child was out of sight, Rachel marched to the sink and filled herself a glass of water, gulped down the contents, then slammed the tumbler onto the counter and glared at the composed Ben.

"Don't you think you were too harsh, Rachel?" he remarked casually.

"I do not. Meggie must learn that it is wrong to maneuver people to her liking. She's just a child. What's *your* excuse for making a spectacle out of yourself and me in front of my neighbors?"

"I hardly think a little friendly bidding for a good cause is a dastardly act. Which upsets you most—that I ruffled your fancy gentleman friend's feathers, or that I escaped being poisoned by your chicken?" Ben retaliated more strongly than he'd intended because he didn't like being scolded in the same way as Meggie and because he sensed that Rachel's accusation was not entirely justified.

"Go to hell" was her unchristianlike comeback as she moved to sweep past him.

He caught her by the shoulders, waylaying her haughty exit. "I've been there once, and I didn't much care for the accommodations, although the company wasn't half bad," he taunted, wanting to shake her and, insanely, longing to kiss her at the same time. "At least my fellow sinners weren't fine, upstanding Christian hypocrites."

Her almond eyes flashed as she struggled to wrench free of his viselike grip. "I'm no hypocrite, Ben Eaton."

He held her tighter, so tight that she couldn't dodge the unexpected descent of his mouth. "Oh, yes you are,

73

Miz Daniels. Because you're very capable of publicly denying private needs for the sake of propriety."

His mouth hovered a breath away from hers—the delectable mouth that was arousing the desire of which he spoke. In spite of herself, she trembled at the prospect of being soundly kissed by Ben Eaton. "I readily admit that I have my weaknesses." She fought to keep her composure, but the breathless quality of her voice betrayed her. To meet his engulfing eyes would be impossible, for then he would surely read the longing within her own. "But I try to do what's decent, Ben. God knows I don't always succeed, but I damned sure try."

The sincerity of her admission and the vulnerability he felt beneath his fingertips made Ben check himself. His clench upon her supple flesh relaxed, and he stepped back from the reckless urge that had seized him. "Giving in to a healthy need now and then isn't necessarily indecent, Rachel. But I certainly respect your right to decline." Without a backward glance, he left her wondering if he'd actually intended to kiss her and fantasizing about the sensuous outcome if he had followed through on his intention. Ben Eaton had given one grownup woman plenty to think about tonight.

CHAPTER FIVE

In the following weeks, as the drought continued, Ben Eaton learned that the widow Daniels was more unpredictable than the fickle rain. Although she gave the appearance of being as strong as hickory, she had lapses when her sensitivity, femininity, and vulnerability seeped through the tough veneer.

One such occasion was the morning after the Box Supper Auction. Ben awoke to discover Meggie tickling his feet and giggling.

"Wake up, lazybones. Mama says we're going to have a picnic lunch over at Armadillo Pond."

Still groggy from a restless night's sleep, he mumbled something unintelligible and yanked the sheet over his head.

Meggie, of course, would not be so easily dismissed. "Come on—you gotta get up," she pestered, tugging at the sheet and prodding him with none-too-gentle shoves.

"It's Sunday. Aren't you supposed to be in church?"

"Mama says we don't have to. We're going fishing for Old Black Joe instead." She wrestled with Napoleon at the foot of the bed and told Ben about the day's itinerary. Between the bed rocking and Napoleon's barking, he had no choice but to rouse himself. He arranged the sheet over his bare limbs, then sat on the edge of the bed, realizing that it was barely daybreak. "Who in the heck is Old Black Joe?" he managed to ask.

"Just the biggest catfish in Texas is all." Meggie scampered to his side, dangling her legs and wiggling her toes. "He's been around since before old Annie Baird was born, and he's got whiskers out to here." She stretched her arms wide. At Ben's disbelieving look, she confirmed the rumor with a sincere, "It's the truth. Even Mama says it's so. And you know what else?"

"There's more?" Ben teased, tweaking her pug nose.

"He's got powers," she murmured in a confidential tone. "He's slicker than a slide that's been dusted with dirt. Folks have hooked him once or twice, but nobody's ever landed him. He wiggles his tail, snaps the line, and disappears like a ghost."

"Is that a fact?" Ben rubbed his stubbled cheek, feigning respectful awe.

"Yup. Mama says Old Black Joe is a legend around here. She thinks we ought to leave him be, but I want to catch him and have a catfish fry."

"You're a mercenary little thing, aren't you?" Ben grinned in spite of himself.

Not quite sure what *mercenary* meant but sensing that it was not a compliment, Meggie scooted off the bed with an indifferent, "Naw. I just want to eat him so I can have powers, too. Hurry and get ready, Ben. You know Mama don't like to be kept waiting. Yo, Napoleon, let's go get Old Black Joe." At the clap of her hands, the feeble Doberman slid off the bed and limped out the door with her.

Ben knew perfectly well that it was Margaret Jane who did not want to be kept waiting. He readied himself posthaste for the fishing expedition to Armadillo Pond. It would be a pleasant respite from the usual Sunday doldrums around the farm—pleasant and totally unexpected, especially after the confrontation with Rachel the night before. The widow Daniels sure could keep a man off balance. Sharp rebukes and sweet shudders at night; a peace offering in the form of a picnic—while breaking one of the Ten Commandments—the next day. Yes, Rachel Daniels was a peculiar woman, all right.

If he lived to be a hundred like Old Black Joe, Ben would never forget that Sunday afternoon excursion to Armadillo Pond. For it was then that he witnessed the side of Rachel Daniels that would become indelibly ingrained in his heart forever.

That day, she was more than congenial, more than pretty, more than wise, more than his heart could ignore. That day, Bennett Earl Eaton III began to fall in love with the woman who had earned his respect and aroused his libido but had not made him wish to seriously contend for her affections.

He had never seen her so carefree. They had never talked so freely. Rachel Daniels had more than stamina; she had substance. She still had her strict principles, her code of "decent" behavior, her old-fashioned values, but she also had a bright mind, a quick wit, and an easy, melodious laugh. She was proud, yet not too proud to admit it when she was wrong. The picnic was her way of making amends for unduly chastising both himself and Meggie the night before.

As they sat in the willow grass by the serene pond, the breeze sifting through her blond hair, she spoke of basics —how precious children were, how grand daybreak was, how lonely the nights could be, what she considered to be petty frustrations and great blessings, how essential it was to have quality in life, not quality measured in dollars and cents but in principle and reciprocated love. And she listened so well, not judgmentally but genuinely interested in his point of view. Warmth like that of the hot August sun emanated from her.

Watching her rebait Meggie's cane pole, Ben couldn't help thinking about the great differences between Rachel and his ex-wife. He had wanted children, and he had thought that whether to have them was not an issue. Not until just before his divorce did Jeanette tell him the truth —that she had undergone a sterilization long before their marriage because the prospect of a pregnancy was abhorrent to her. Odd that he should know Rachel better in one afternoon than he knew his ex-wife in all their years of marriage. Funnier still, he was tempted to risk talking to Rachel of the past, which he'd never discussed with another soul. He chose not to, though, partly because of pride, partly because he simply didn't want to blemish the mood with his bitterness.

True to form, Rachel had not exactly prepared a feast for them. But peanut butter and jelly sandwiches, potato chips, and Twinkies had never tasted so good. He confessed that he suspected her of holding out on him when it came to mealtimes. She merely grinned, neither confirming nor denying his suspicion.

She suggested that Meggie take time out from trying to catch Old Black Joe to play a game of Blind Man's Bluff with them. Meggie thought the game was great fun, but it was Ben who thoroughly enjoyed the ruse. With a bandanna tied around her eyes, Rachel came upon him, hands outstretched, feeling for her quarry. He would never know if it was only for Meggie's benefit or also for her own that Rachel took an inordinate amount of time to identify her prisoner. The stroke of her gentle palms along his face, shoulders, chest, and arms was electric. He sensed it was for her, too.

Just when he thought he couldn't withstand her touch any longer without reciprocating or groaning, she laughed gaily and stated coyly, "Why, I believe it must be Ben that I've snared. Aha! I'm right! I've captured, Ben." To Meggie's delight, he growled like Benny the teddy bear, locked Rachel in his arms, and swung the blindfolded taunter around.

Had she ever captured him! She felt perfect, he thought, as if she'd been born to be cloaked in his arms. She flung off the bandanna and for a flitting but poignant moment he saw longing in her bright eyes. It was enough to make him wonder if he might have a chance with her.

Meggie, however, had other fish to fry, or so she hoped. She had lost interest in the game and once again was stalking Old Black Joe with her cane pole. Rachel was packing up the picnic trappings and Ben had just finished recounting the details of the wager he'd entered into with Bubba Atkins when Meggie let out a blood-curdling yelp. She had snagged the infamous catfish and was struggling to tug him ashore. Reflexively, Ben rushed to help her. After a few tense minutes and innumerable instructions from Meggie, he banked the huge fish.

"I got him! He's mine! And I did it all by myself!" Meggie whooped.

Rachel came over to see about the commotion. On seeing Old Black Joe flopping pathetically on the bank, she dropped to her knees beside the catfish and beckoned Meggie to her side.

"Aren't you proud of me, Mama?" Meggie had asked with no modesty whatever.

Rachel's arm slipped around the child's waist, and she drew her closer, smoothing her wild curls and saying, "Yes, of course I'm proud of you. Catching Old Black Joe is quite a feat. The question is, do you really want to keep him, sweetheart? He'll die if you don't put him back in Armadillo Pond."

"But if I do that, nobody will believe I caught him," Meggie protested. "Dory Phillips will swear that I made the whole thing up."

Rachel smiled patiently. "But you know better, Meggie. Old Black Joe is a part of Armadillo Pond. It's his home, where he lives and breathes. He can't exist anywhere else. It's necessary to him. And in a way, he's necessary to us. He's part of our heritage."

"What's a heritage?" the child had asked.

"It's what makes you what you are, honey. It's the land, the trees, the house you grew up in, the people who touch your life, and the stories you've heard a hundred times, like the legend of Old Black Joe. If he no longer existed, children wouldn't know of his power and old men wouldn't come to nap by the pond to catch a glimpse of him. It's important to hang on to our heritage, for it nourishes our soul, just like food fills our hunger."

Ben knew what Rachel spoke of, knew the terrible void that losing one's heritage left. How simply Rachel had expressed such an intangible asset as identity. He shouldn't have been astounded, but he was—astounded and deeply touched.

"Quick, Ben, help me put him back," Meggie beseeched, bending and attempting to extract the hook. "He doesn't look so good. We gotta hurry."

He brushed aside Meggie's hands and adeptly removed the hook from the catfish's mouth. In a flash and a splash, Old Black Joe was once more in his natural habitat. As Meggie waved good-bye to him, Ben and Rachel exchanged glances. They both knew the symbolic importance of Old Black Joe's continued existence, but they also both knew that the rain that still had not come was vital to their own. In two weeks, Ben would win the bet with Bubba, even as the threat of a crop-gutting, heritage-abolishing drought became more real with each passing day. More than ever, he was determined to do all that was humanly possible to save the Daniels farm from extinction.

The blazing heat persisted with no relief from the heavens. Already sorely taxed, soon the irrigating sources would be dry. In the ensuing days, Ben often spied Rachel's silhouette at sunset, standing at the edge of the fields and gazing wistfully up at the sky in search of a sign of rain. Only once or twice—and then only in the form of a passing casual comment—had she shared her concern with him. He admired her immensely for her uncomplaining nature, and he envied her unquestioning faith in a benevolent Almighty. How he wished he could believe in the miracle of divine intervention! But he'd been tested and deprived of any such hope, and he had no faith left.

What he did have was an extra hundred dollars in his pocket, since Bubba Atkins had lost the wager. As he watched Rachel stroll across the fields and inspect the parched cotton crop, a rash but compelling thought seized him. Rachel needed a break from the tension, and he had the means to provide one—something spontaneous and mending, like a relaxing ride to Dallas for a fine meal and her favorite Irish coffee. He knew just the place, refined yet cozy, with an exquisite view of the city. It would be a replenishing diversion for them both.

The trick was to convince Rachel to accept his invitation. She'd balk at the suggestion and would have a score of excuses for why the jaunt would be impossible—Meggie, the crops, the cost, the unseemliness of it, and so forth. He'd just have to be persuasive and offer countering solutions to her arguments. Something told him that this brief respite from their arduous routine and anxieties was more than just a whim; it was a healing necessity. Even a woman as strong as Rachel had her limit. Even a man as disillusioned as he was had a dream or two left.

Even after the six-hour drive to Dallas, as he sat across the linen-draped table from Rachel watching her read the extensive menu, Ben still did not quite grasp how he had managed to persuade her to accept his invitation. Perhaps it was luck, or fate, or whatever label one applied to a boon. But regardless of the reason for Rachel's unexpected acceptance, he was pleased to have the opportunity to spend some private time with her—uninterrupted hours with no minor crop crisis or major intrusion like Jonas McMurtry's dropping by to infringe upon their holiday. He couldn't help thinking that adjectives like *lovely* and *svelte* were pale descriptions of her today. She looked sensational, and he wondered how he could take her comeliness for granted most of the time. Of course, the fact that she had traded in her standard bibbed overalls and paisley bandanna for a silk turquoise sheath and matching hair ornaments might explain his heightened awareness.

"These prices are sky high, Ben. Surely Bubba's losses weren't as much as this. Maybe we should consider a more modest restaurant."

He smiled at her well-intentioned proposal. Little did she know, there was a time in his life when he'd wined and dined a multitude of business associates in this very same restaurant. The staff had changed, the prices had increased, and the elite clientele was now comprised of newer and younger executives out to impress and make their mark on the corporate world. Much was different, all right. Yesterday he had been like the Halston-clad yuppies with unlimited credit cards; today he was an ordinary Joe whom the snooty waiter had instantly assessed to be out of his realm.

"Order whatever you like, Rachel. We're splurging today, compliments of the foolhardy Bubba," he assured her.

"You're sure?"

"Positive. You should try the Crême Vichyssoise as an appetizer. It's excellent," he suggested knowledgeably.

At that revealing slip, Rachel set aside her menu and studied him. From the moment they had entered the elite dining room, she'd sensed what he had just confirmed—that Ben Eaton was no stranger to these plush surroundings. He was neither ill at ease nor awed, as she was. It was almost as if he were accustomed to such sophistication! He was wearing the raw silk suit and monogrammed shirt that always aroused her curiosity. And now he was making food and wine selections that she couldn't even pronounce. No, Ben Eaton was not unfamiliar with the so-called good life. Fine clothes and haute cuisine had once figured significantly in his background.

She was brimming with unanswered questions, but she only asked one. "How long has it been since you were here last, Ben?"

The smile faded from his lips, and he, too, set aside his menu. "Several years." At least his scant answer was honest. "Are you ready to order?"

"I'll let you do the honors—only don't choose anything too rich. I'm not the fishy-suave sort." The remark was uncalled for, and the second she said it she wished she could retract it.

Ben's features did not betray him. It was hard for him to ignore her sarcasm and mispronunciation, but during the last few years he'd had a lot of practice swallowing his pride and suppressing his emotions. He signaled the waiter and placed an order for prime rib, baked potato, salad, and red wine. Rachel did not know how rare or costly the wine was. He preferred it that way.

As soon as the waiter departed, she apologized for her rudeness. "I'm sorry I said that. It's just that sometimes we speak different languages, and I wonder if we truly communicate at all. We live under the same roof, share the same food, work side by side from dawn to dusk, and yet . . ." She shrugged and stared down at her lap.

"And yet you feel we're strangers at times," he supplied.

"Not strangers exactly—just not good friends," she corrected.

The waiter brought the wine, and Ben sampled the vintage, then nodded his approval. After filling Rachel's glass, the waiter left.

She sipped the wine, thinking it was very good indeed. "Good friends don't keep things from one another, Ben. You know practically everything about my life, while I can only guess about yours before we met. All I know is that you once lived in Dallas, were married, and have an aversion to discussing yourself. Why is that? You make me think there is some terrible dark secret in your past."

He grinned ruefully. "I'm not a mass murderer or a political dissident, if that's what you mean."

In spite of herself, she had to smile. "I hardly thought so. But I do believe you once led an entirely different life-style than you do now. You're not rural America, and you're not a drifter by choice."

"No, I'm not," he confessed, taking a hefty swig of the

wine. "I've wanted to talk to you about myself, Rachel, but either the timing was wrong or my pride got in the way. You must understand. It's hard for a man to speak of—"

"Well, I'll be damned." A sound slap on his back took Ben completely off guard. "I thought these old eyes of mine were playing tricks, but it *is* you, Earl Eaton, in the flesh! How the heck are you?" His former business associate pumped his hand.

Ben stood from his chair. "I'm doing fine, Mark."

"Glad to hear it. The way you dropped out of circulation, I wondered if maybe you'd fallen off the face of the earth. I was really sorry to hear about your string of bad luck. Damn shame about the breakup between you and Jeanette. Some of us had our doubts that you would weather the setbacks," the man commiserated.

"Well, as you can see, I survived." Wishing to distract the associate from blurting out any more of his private affairs, Ben extricated his hand and introduced him to Rachel. "This is Rachel Daniels."

"Nice to meet you, Miss Daniels." The distinguished-looking gentleman nodded politely.

She acknowledged him with a similar dip of her head.

"Well, I didn't mean to intrude on your supper. Will you be in town long?"

Rachel now knew his ex-wife's name and what B.E.E. stood for. Part of the mystery of Ben Eaton had been solved. Yet she sensed it was just the tip of the iceberg. A great deal still remained unknown to her about her hired hand.

"Only for today," Ben replied, retaking his seat.

"Too bad. I would've liked to buy you a drink at the Petroleum Club for old times' sake. Get in touch the next time you're in Dallas, and we'll have lunch."

"I'll do that." Ben almost sounded as if he meant it.

After the former acquaintance departed and the waiter had served their meal, the silence between Ben and Rachel became exaggerated. Finally, Ben broke the strained reticence.

"People knew me as Earl Eaton here in Dallas," he explained.

"So I gathered," she said between bites, feigning a nonchalance she did not possess.

"I do want to tell you about myself, Rachel, and I guess this is as good a time as there will ever be."

The pain in his eyes made her wish the recounting of his past were not necessary. But it was. She had to unravel the mystery of the stranger who had once belonged to exclusive clubs and now lived in exile outside of Lubbock. What series of setbacks had so drastically altered his status that he had been led to her humble doorstep? She couldn't help yearning for details, any more than she could help lying awake nights fantasizing about a physical encounter with him. During the main course, dessert, and several Irish coffees, she came to know the man called Earl Eaton.

Once he had been one of the biggest oil magnates in Dallas and had ruled over an empire that had been passed down from generation to generation. He was the sole heir to a legacy of privilege and fortune. Power was the inalienable right of a man like him. Naturally, he had married a beautiful socialite who knew everything about voguish entertaining and nothing about hardship or perseverance.

When his empire had threatened to collapse due to speculative ventures before the oil glut, his associates had bailed out, and not a banker in the country would lend him assistance. After exhausting every avenue of financial aid, he had been forced to declare bankruptcy. And after he had ceased to be the oil czar of Dallas, his friends no longer extended invitations, his wife no longer wished to share his life or name, and his family labeled him an embarrassment and no longer claimed him. He became a man without alternatives or hope or identity.

It had been easy to lose himself in the back roads of the country, where his once-prestigious name meant nothing. He had traveled extensively, only stopping off at various points to work at menial jobs for minimal wages whenever his funds ran dry. All the fine things that had been second nature to him did not matter anymore. Nothing mattered anymore. That was what became of the man who suddenly found himself without a heritage. That was why a struggling widow trying to cling to her roots could have an impact on him and make him want to help her.

Rachel reached across the table and took his hand in hers. Her compassionate touch was almost more than he could bear. "I didn't tell you about myself to elicit sympathy, Rachel." His voice sounded hollow—depleted—starkly unlike him.

"I'm only offering my thanks for finally sharing your past with me. I understand you a lot better now." She squeezed his hand, and when he could finally bring himself to lift his resigned eyes, he was heartened by her sweet smile.

"The last thing I wanted was for you to be burdened today," he said. "Maybe returning to Dallas wasn't such a good idea after all. It must bring up some old memories for you, too." He felt her hand tense, then relax again.

"It's been a nice evening. One of the best I can remember in a long time. I thank you for it, Ben Eaton."

"You're most welcome." Try as he might, he couldn't disguise the quaver in his voice.

"I think we ought to be heading back, though. It'll be late before we get home." She withdrew her hand and finished the Irish coffee.

He was amazed at how much he missed her touch. "Whatever you want, Rachel," he acceded, reluctantly signaling the waiter for the check.

It was almost midnight by the time they arrived back at the farm. Meggie was spending the night with Dory, and the old house seemed to groan with emptiness. Ben lingered on the back porch to smoke a cheroot and collect his thoughts before retiring. Damn, but he wished it would rain! Even the late-night air was so dry, it singed the lungs to breathe it.

He paced restlessly, inhaling on the cheroot and exhaling the smoke into the quiet night. He felt frustrated and hot and excruciatingly lonely. A vulnerable part of him wished Rachel had not become so intimate during the dinner, for now he sorely wanted what was not possible. He could imagine it, though. In his mind, he envisioned making love to her. The image made his loins ache, his adrenaline rise, and his agitated steps quicken. He'd probably paced a good two miles by the time she appeared on the porch.

"Would you like another toddy before bed?" Her voice was mellow and the feminine sway of her hips was almost hypnotic as she came near to where he roosted on the porch railing.

I want you, his secret self yearned. "I'll pass."

She nodded, hugging the railing post with an arm and gazing dreamily up at the star-studded sky. "Do you think it might rain tomorrow?" She was trying hard to be casual, not to let him perceive the almost-tangible desire she felt. Never in her life had she experienced such a strong attraction to a man. For the first time ever, she understood the gravitational pull of the sun on the earth and the moon's on the tide. Such was the effect Ben Eaton's quiet charisma had on her. She'd been fighting it for months, but tonight, after discovering what a fascinating man he actually was, her defenses were weakened. In fact, tonight she was as susceptible to his body heat as the arid earth was to the scorching sun.

He stared blankly into space, answering automatically, and repressed his urge to confess that he craved her as the cotton crop thirsted for rain. "If not tomorrow, soon," he predicted.

She dismissed the stars and concentrated on him instead. "What would I have done these past few months without your strong back and encouragement to rely on?"

He was stunned by the compliment. As he turned and met her soulful brown eyes, he almost found the courage to tell her that he could become even more necessary if she would let him. "You're a resourceful woman, Rachel. You'd have found the strength to make it through."

"Probably. But you shouldered part of my load without complaint or pay, and I am grateful. I wish there were some way I could show my appreciation." She also wished he would read the entreaty in her eyes and the invitation in her words. She stepped nearer—near enough to detect his cologne. Her senses were acutely aware of how wholly masculine he was and how greatly she missed the smell, the sound, the touch, and the feel of a man.

His arms ached to enfold her. His lips could almost taste hers. She'd be sweet, so goddamned sweet. His body tensed at her approach, and he hastily ground out his cheroot with his boot. "There is something I would like from you, Rachel," he heard himself saying.

The moonlight spilled over her lovely face as she came

still closer. Her sultry lips shimmered like faint starlight as she answered, "If it's within my power to give . . ."

It was. Before sanity returned, before she could renege, he caught her about the waist by an arm, forged her body to his, and kissed her as if he had the right to. To his amazement, she did not resist. Instead, she responded with hunger that equaled his own. He dared to kiss her more deeply, embrace her more tightly. Her hands cradled the back of his neck as his tongue searched the moist region beyond her answering lips. Unafraid, eager to please, her body instinctively molded itself to him—supple breasts to hard chest, firm thighs to muscular ones.

It had been so long since he'd held or kissed a woman, and yet it was not the prospect of the end of abstinence that excited him—it was Rachel herself. She kissed like an angel, and her body beckoned like a seductress's. He had never encountered a woman quite like her. If this were a prelude to her lovemaking, he might not survive the actual act. He might very well die from the sheer ecstasy of it. He forced himself to retreat, running his splayed fingers through her rich hair and smiling forlornly. "I should apologize for that." He found it difficult to sound sincere.

"It's not necessary." Limply, she leaned against him. In all her years with Yancy, she had never felt so weak or so satisfied.

"You're a very special woman, Rachel. You deserve to be treated with respect and regard." Gently, he stroked her back, marveling at how complex a creature she was—fragile yet resilient, and so utterly desirable.

She lifted her blond head and gazed deep into his smoky eyes. "You do want me, don't you, Ben?"

A lump formed in his throat. He swallowed hard and admitted, "Yes, Rachel. I won't deny it. I want to carry you upstairs and make love to you until we're both exhausted."

The dimples he so adored materialized with her smile. "Then do," she said simply.

He could hardly believe it, but he was not about to ignore her blanket permission. Wordlessly, he swooped her up into his arms and marched to the back door. She helped his amorous pilgrimage by opening that one barrier to their union. Through the kitchen, up the stairs, into her bedroom, and onto the bed, they kissed. Not a word was exchanged; only seeking looks, exploring strokes, and sensual currents passed between them as they undressed one another, discovered one another, savored one another. For Rachel, he was every bit as appealing and virile as she had imagined. For Ben, she was as perfectly proportioned and warmly dispositioned as he had believed. For them both, this act was not impulsive or alien. No, it was natural and easy and divine.

He strung kisses along her neck, the hollow of her throat, the slender curve of her shoulders, the enticing swell of her ivory breasts, and murmured, "It's been a long time since I've been with a woman. If I'm greedy, forgive me."

She raked her tapered nails through his thick hair, then massaged the nape of his neck and the wide bridge of his sleek back, sighing. "I've done without, too, Ben. Be as greedy as you like, because I will be, too." And that was no idle threat.

Wantonly, her hands traveled over his magnificent body until she knew every sinewy curve of him, every manly swell of him. He felt as delicious beneath her fingertips as he tasted beneath her lips. She devoured his sensuality, arousing her own. Her tempo became feverish as her passion climbed. The silent love song she played upon his flesh made his heart drum wildly, as if to the beat of a bolero. Where had she learned such eroticism? he wondered. Or was she just naturally uninhibited and incredibly sexy?

He had to take control or risk a premature end to their intimacy. He maneuvered her onto her back, capturing her delicate wrists and delectable mouth. "Slower, honey, slower," he crooned. Masterfully, he straddled her and sought the sensitive region between her trembling thighs. Gradually, he claimed what had once belonged to another but now, tonight, was his and his alone.

Her hips writhed, and she moaned in pleasure. He thrust slowly, and she yearned greatly, trying to absorb him as the needy cotton would gulp the rain. He bent his head to her aroused breasts, sampling first one budded nipple then the other.

She arched, whispering hoarsely, "I can't stand it. Please, please . . ."

He inched deeper but conserved himself, wanting to prolong and escalate her imminent climax. "You're so lovely, Rachel . . . so desirable." His lips brushed hers. "You feel so damned good," he rasped, withdrawing slightly as his thumb sought out the most private and sensitive place on a woman's body. Expertly, he massaged and aroused her to the point of no return.

"Ben, oh, God, Ben," she moaned feverishly, undulating to the rhythm he set and grazing her palms along his silky, matted chest.

With extraordinary patience and power he satisfied her, forging himself deep into the nirvana of her womanliness. "Don't move," he gasped. "Let's linger for as long as we can."

"I want to . . . I do," she murmured deliriously, "but

I can't. I need you now!" The whole of her body shuddered with sweet anticipation.

The effect was like a tidal wave, and the two surged, then spilled over the euphoric precipice at the same instant. It was the most intense, most frightening, most gratifying experience of their lives. Shaken and satisfied, they clung to each other until their distorted senses cleared.

He gathered her into his arms and held her tightly against him. His sigh came from deep within and expressed a volume of feelings. She cuddled closer to his warm and reassuringly solid body, pressing her lips to his cheek. "I haven't had much practice at lingering," she confessed.

He smiled broadly, easing her back onto the pillow and smoothing the tumbled wisps of hair from her face. "Neither have I. It's just that you are so incredibly sweet, and I hated for it to end."

Her almond eyes glowed with reciprocal admiration as she slipped her hands into his hair and brought his mouth to hers. "With a little more practice, I could learn the knack of lingering," she said breathily against his lips.

Not only did he kiss her again and again, but throughout the wee small hours he made love to her again and again. They did not examine why they were in bed together this night; they did not discuss the future of other nights. They merely acted on feelings that they had yet to think through. Tomorrow they would consider the reasons and repercussions. Tonight, Ben and Rachel shared only their pent-up passion and great need.

CHAPTER SIX

The morning after and the days following were a little tense and a lot uncomfortable. Everything still appeared to be normal on the surface and the daily routine went on as usual, but beneath the casual facade brewed doubts and unrest.

Rachel found herself reliving that night with Ben a hundred times in her mind. It remained so vivid that often, as she lay in bed, she would think he was there, reaching for her, touching her. The sensation seemed so real that it would cause her to bolt upright. She missed him that intensely, much too much, but she did her damnedest not to let it show.

She was self-conscious around him now, constantly wondering what he must think of her. What she imagined was not complimentary, and she looked for excuses to avoid contact with him. Instead of sitting on the back porch or at the kitchen table keeping him company in the evenings, she stayed apart and kept busy with chores.

Her uneasiness was apparent. Her reasons were not. Ben could not know the struggle that waged inside her, especially when she was taking such pains to hide it from him. Before Ben left her bed that night after the Dallas trip, she'd known she had come to care for him more than a woman who professed to be self-sufficient should.

It hadn't been only a strong physical thing between them or mild fondness. Either of those she could've accepted and handled. What she couldn't deal with was the void after he returned to his own room. He took a part of her with him—the impractical part that would have denied the impulse to throw her arms around him, draw him back into bed, pull the covers over their heads, and say to hell with responsibility and independence.

Yancy's death had not threatened the confidence she had in her ability to cope alone. But Ben's departure did. He made her want to shun what was unpleasant and cling to him. He made her want to escape in his expert lovemaking. He made her want to hoard his tenderness. He made the widow want to love the drifter. But this she could not do. It went against her grain. She was a woman or permanence and small-town values. Ben Eaton possessed neither. He was temporary, of a world so vastly different that it was unlikely they'd find common ground on which to build a lasting relationship.

More than once as she watched him in the field, working so hard and looking so fine, she wondered how she'd be able to stand another lonely night without him. Only a staircase separated them. It would be so easy to tiptoe down to his room and crawl into his bed. It would be so wonderful to have him satisfy her need once more. In the dark his impermanence wouldn't matter. Under the covers she could not see the distant horizons shimmering in his eyes. But in the light of day she could clearly perceive the outcome. In spite of herself she would fall deeply in love with Ben Eaton, and it would break her heart when he traveled on. No, it was better not to give in to the temptation. She had to try to forget the way he moved so right and satisfied her every desire. For as surely as September would become October and the summer cotton fields would be replanted with winter wheat, Ben Eaton would be gone from Mesquite Junction, drifting with the wind and leaving a memory in his stead. She knew she'd never entirely forget a man as remarkable as he, but at least she wouldn't grieve for him. Better to maintain her distance, to reestablish their boundaries. Better to want him in silence than to love him at such cost.

That was Rachel's reasoning, and that was her ever constant turmoil. Ben's frustration was even worse. He didn't understand why she had withdrawn from him. Over and over again, he replayed the night of their love-making in his head. She had been so loving and responsive. She had seemed so content when he had left her. For the life of him he could not figure out what had occurred between dawn and breakfast the next morning to change things. But as surely as the weather remained constant, without a sign of rain, Rachel reverted back to her disciplined self, without a sign of encouragement for him. Her hot-then-cold manner baffled him.

At first, he thought it was just a front she put up for Meggie's sake. But soon he realized that Rachel was going to great lengths to avoid anything personal between them. But there were times when he'd catch her by surprise with a smile or a wink, and he'd evoke a flicker of genuine affection in her eyes. And there were the moments when she came to say good night. He knew he wasn't imagining the hesitation and the tension in her voice. She was trying hard not to become involved. But why? he asked himself day in and day out. What had he done to make Rachel so guarded?

At night he lay awake remembering that hot August night and yearning to be with her again. He thought about taking the initiative and shocking her into submission. But what would he gain? Rachel was the sort of woman who had to come to terms with things at her own pace. He suspected that old-fashioned embarrassment played a part in altering her manner. He wanted to reassure her that he still held her in the highest regard. But he knew that if he even tried to broach the subject, she would retreat even more.

It was driving him crazy, and he was certain that she, too, was a nervous wreck. Between the persistent heat and the constant tension, they were both on edge. The farm was like a powder keg. It couldn't go on; something had to give. He was almost sorry they had made love at all. Had he abstained, he would've never known how sweet she was and he would not be craving her like a child craves candy.

Because she wasn't a woman who gave herself easily to a man, he knew there had to be some feeling for him on her part. It was still there; he sensed it. He just didn't know how to break down the wall she had erected.

He had never intended to complicate her life. Yet he obviously had. He wanted so much to hold her, to tell her again how special she was, and to make whatever was wrong between them right.

At one point he had tried. She had lost her footing climbing down from the back of the pickup, and he'd caught her around the waist to break her fall. For a suspended moment, they stood pinned together, and he could feel the erratic pounding of her heart. Their eyes locked, and he saw inexplicable panic.

"For God's sake, what's wrong, Rachel?" he had asked. But just then, Meggie had come hobbling up, crying to Rachel about a freshly scraped knee. The opportunity was lost as she swiftly extricated herself from his arms to tend to her daughter.

The tension was contagious. Even Meggie was cranky

lately. Sensing the dissention and unable to pinpoint the cause, in her childish innocence she blamed herself for the general bad mood about the farm.

"I think Mama's upset. Did she say anything to you about Miz Phillips coming by to have a word with her?" The jam-faced tot dragged the toe of her sandal through the dirt as Ben was unloading several boxes of shingles from the pickup. He had just returned from a trip to McMurtry's Seed and Supply and was a little preoccupied with jealous thoughts about Jonas and Rachel. Something about the way the smug son of a bitch had said "Tell Rachel I'll put this on her account and not to worry herself about it being past due. We'll work something out" made Ben's blood boil.

"Not that I remember." His short reply did little to alleviate Meggie's troubled conscience. She tagged close behind as Ben strode into the barn to gather a hammer and roofing nails.

"Well, if she hasn't, she will."

"Who will what?" He'd already forgotten her reference to Dory Phillips's mother. Haphazardly, he searched amid the clutter on the work bench for the missing hammer.

Meggie ducked under his arms, shoved aside a torn kite, and located the evasive tool. "Miz Phillips, that's who. And I betcha she's already told Mama what I did. That's why she's been so moody. She's probably debating about sending me off to one of those schools for bad children." Meggie handed him the hammer. Her large brown eyes were full of guilt and fret.

Realizing that the child truly thought herself the source of her mother's bad humor and that she was fearful of the consequences, Ben set aside the hammer and his own concerns to give Meggie his undivided attention.

He mustered a patient smile, took a seat on a concrete block, and patted his knee. Like a lickety-split chipmunk, she scampered up into his lap and snuggled her curly head against his chest.

"Now, what's all this nonsense about being exiled to a school for bad children?" he coaxed.

"I did a terrible thing, Ben. I suppose the devil made me do it." She hadn't yet told him the dastardly deed but was already supplying an excuse for it. "Miz Phillips was real mad. She said I was a brat and needed a sound licking."

His curiosity piqued, Ben could hardly wait to hear the woeful tale. "Why don't you back up and tell me what exactly it is that you did?"

Meggie gnawed her bottom lip and looked up at him beguilingly. "First you gotta understand how bossy Dory is. She never wants to play anything but dress-up and beauty shop."

"And you don't like to play sissy stuff like that," he prodded.

"Naw. I like to play astronauts and bottlecaps best." She perked a little straighter in his lap. "Well, crummy Dory tricked me into playing beauty shop with her all afternoon. She said if we did what she wanted first, then she'd play bottlecaps after supper."

"But when it came time to do what you wanted, she changed her mind," he supplied.

"Yup. She said she was just teasing me and wasn't gonna play dumb old bottlecaps. Stuck out her tongue and went to watch TV. She wouldn't even share her Popsicle."

Ben showed the appropriate amount of sympathy. "I suppose that is more than enough to warrant some sort of retaliation."

"I didn't want to retattle! I just wanted to get even."
She swung her shorts-clad legs to and fro. "So I waited
till Dory went to sleep that night and I played beauty
shop—but good."

Ben was beginning to fear the worst and wasn't at all
sure he wanted to hear the gory details anymore. "I really hope you didn't do what I think you did."

"Are you thinking that I took the scissors and
whacked off Dory's hair?" She clicked her sandals together and stared at her bare tootsies.

Aghast and amused, he didn't dare risk a comment.

"Well, I did," she admitted with only a smidgeon of
remorse. "When she woke up and saw it, she started
bawling, and then Miz Phillips came busting into the
room and started turning purple. She said she was gonna
tell Mama first chance she got. And I figure she did, and
Mama's so ashamed of me that she doesn't want to talk
about it. Why else would she be thinking so hard and not
smiling much a'tall?"

Although Meggie deserved to be reprimanded for
shearing Dory Phillips, he hated for her to draw the
wrong conclusion about her mother's recent preoccupation. "I don't think your mother's mood has anything to
do with what you did at Dory's. And even if Miz Phillips
has spoken to her"—Meggie winced—"and I feel certain
she hasn't yet"—her anxiousness ebbed some—"I know
for certain that your mama wouldn't send you to juvenile
detention, though a paddling isn't out of the realm of
possibility." He swung her off his lap and stood. "It's just
that your mother has a lot on her mind right now, Meggie. She's worried about the crop and other things. You
and I must be patient with her. She'll be her old self soon.
Count on it." Playfully, he ruffed her mop of wild curls.

The explanation seemed to ease Meggie's mind only

minimally. Her little legs trotted double time to keep up with Ben as he shouldered a ladder and walked outside the barn. "Are you gonna tell her what I did before Miz Phillips gets the chance?"

He paused, then reassured her with a pinch of her cheek, "I'm no snitch, Margaret Jane. If I were you, I'd tell your mother myself. Keeping secrets, especially bad ones, wears on a person. You'll feel better once you fess up."

"But she'll throw a hissy-fit and hate me forever," she protested.

"The best part about mothers, honey, is that they'll love you no matter what." And with those words of wisdom he hoisted the ladder and walked off toward the house, leaving the rascal to mull over her unsavory choices.

It was midafternoon by the time Rachel returned from the fields to the house. She was dumbfounded at the sight of Ben perched atop the roof and Meggie collecting the old shingles he threw to the ground, then depositing them into a large trash sack—dumbfounded and more than a little perturbed.

"Just what the heck do you think you're doing?" she hollered up to him.

He sat back on his haunches and swiped a forearm across his sweaty brow. "I should think it's fairly obvious, Rachel." Dehydrated from the heat and his legs cramped from bracing his weight, he was not in the mood to be third-degreed.

She stood with one hand upon a jutted hip, the other shading her piercing eyes. "I don't remember discussing reroofing the house with you. And would you mind telling me just where and how you bought those new shingles?"

Sensing a royal snit-storm, Meggie dragged the sack of reject shingles to the steps and took a front-row seat for the fireworks.

Ben dug his heels in, partly to keep from sliding down the steep slope, partly to stay himself from pouncing on top of Rachel's haughty figure. It was at least a hundred degrees on the roof, and his patience was wearing thin. "Considering the condition of this roof, Rachel, I thought it was obvious that it needed repair. If and when it ever does rain, this place is going to leak like a sieve unless I replace these rotten shingles."

She was anything but satisfied. "I asked where you got the supplies."

Meggie knew that tone. It meant her mother's chest was becoming blotchy, which meant that she was on the verge of one of her hissy-fits—that wild and totally unreasonable state that she had tried to describe earlier to Ben. Mama didn't lose her poise often, but when she did —oh, brother!

Ben resented her tone. He'd had just about all he was going to take from the unappreciative widow. "I bought the shingles at McMurtry's."

Rachel wanted to scale the roof and strangle the life from him. How dare he make such a major purchase without her approval! "You know damned well I can't afford this! Just how in the Sam Hill am I supposed to pay him?" The blotches were steadily creeping up her neck.

Meggie decided to make herself scarce until things simmered down. Mama was plenty sore, and Ben was literally chewing on the roofing nails in his mouth.

He spat them into his hand and turned his back before

answering, "I wouldn't worry myself too much about it." Ripping another defective shingle from its niche, he slung it over the sagging eave onto the ground at her feet. "If nothing else, I'm sure Jonas would be more than happy to take it out in trade." Ben couldn't help himself. The jealous sarcasm had spilled from his lips before he could think.

Rachel blanched at the insult. Immediately she checked to see if Meggie had overheard the tacky remark, but she had vanished from sight. "For two cents I'd fire your butt, Ben Eaton. If you ever say anything as crude as that to me again, you're history around here. I mean it. You hear me?"

His hammering drowned out not only the threat but the sound of Jonas McMurtry's Jeep coming up the lane. Rachel all but groaned aloud when the dapper Jonas hollered out, "Afternoon, Rachel! Your hired hand forgot a box of shingles when he was in earlier. Since I had an errand to run out this way, I thought I'd deliver them personally."

At Ben's scoffing snort, she forced an appreciative smile and a syrupy welcome. "Why, thank you, Jonas. I hope you can spare the time to share a cool glass of cider with me?"

Parched and beside himself with envy, Ben pried and pounded shingles with a vengeance. He'd like nothing better than to pulverize McMurtry's arrogant face and shake Rachel senseless. Purposely, he shotputted a shingle directly at McMurtry's head. Unfortunately, the dandy stooped to dust off his shoes on the back of his pants leg and missed being decapitated by a split-second.

"Pretty hot up there, I'll bet," Jonas shouted up to him as he marched up the steps.

"Yeah. You might tell Rachel, if it wouldn't put her

out too much, that I could use some of that cool cider myself." He wanted to remind the widow that he was sweating like a pack mule atop her damned roof and had been privy to their every word.

In a few minutes Jonas climbed the ladder and handed him a tumbler of cider without ice cubes. "Rachel said she was sorry but she used the last of the ice in our drinks."

Ben snatched the tumbler from him, muttering, "Tell her thanks a bunch."

Jonas eased down the ladder and went to sit beside Rachel on the porch swing. Up above, Ben sipped the cider and eavesdropped on their conversation.

"I really am beholden to you for the additional credit, Jonas," Rachel said sweetly.

"You know I couldn't refuse you anything you need, Rachel." The porch swing creaked lazily.

"I don't want any special favors. I intend to pay you every dime I owe," she vowed.

"I hate to see you struggling so. You know I want to do all I can to make things easier for you."

Ben could almost see the scene below. Just about now, McMurtry would be slinking his arm around her shoulder to give her a consoling pat. The man was ridiculously predictable and that made him doubly offensive.

From his post atop the roof Ben spied Meggie skipping across the yard. A wry grin broke upon his tanned face. Her timing was absolutely perfect. If McMurtry had any romantic aspirations, Margaret Jane's pesty intrusion would dampen his enthusiasm. "I gotta talk to you, Mama. It's important," he heard Meggie whine.

"Not now, honey. Mr. McMurtry and I are visiting at the moment." Rachel tried to shoo her daughter off.

"But I need to talk right now, Mama. It's kind of private, too," Meggie insisted.

Ben loved it. What a deliciously opportune moment for Meggie to suffer pangs of conscience!

"You're being extremely rude, Margaret Jane," Rachel scolded.

"It's all right, Rachel. We can visit another time. Perhaps next Sunday afternoon? I could come by after church and take you on a picnic to Armadillo Pond," Jonas suggested. He flashed Meggie a toothy smile. "You, too, of course, if you'd like, dumplin'."

"Naw. I don't like picnics much. I'll just hang out around here with Ben," the tot declined. It was an out-and-out excuse, and they all three knew it.

Ben pitched the tumbler below, whistling an inane tune as he began hammering once again.

Rachel was acutely aware of his annoying presence and of Meggie's deliberate impertinence. "I'd love to picnic with you this Sunday, Jonas. In fact, I insist on bringing dessert. I'll fix you something real special. It's the least I can do in return for all your kindnesses."

"Great. I'll be by to pick you up right after the service." He squeezed Rachel's hand and bade Meggie adieu with a tickle of her pouting chin. "See you later, dumplin'."

"Please, let it rain Sunday," Meggie whispered to the Almighty as Jonas climbed into his Jeep and backed onto the blacktopped road. Then her eyes grew as big as saucers when she spied a familiar station wagon braking to let the Jeep pass. Holy moly! It was Miz Phillips come to tattle!

Urgently, she tugged on her mother's overalls. "You gotta listen to me, Mama. There's somethin' I should tell you before Miz Phillips does," she wailed.

"What on earth has gotten into you, Margaret Jane? First you're rude to Mr. McMurtry, and now you're behaving like a babbling monkey! I swear you're trying my patience lately. Do not, under any circumstances, interrupt Miz Phillips. I will deal with whatever it is after she has gone. Understand me?" Rachel crossed her arms and tapped her foot.

"Yes, ma'am," the child uttered, shrinking behind her mother as Miz Phillips wrestled her rotund body from behind the steering wheel and waddled up to the porch.

"Nice to see you, Henrietta," Rachel greeted.

"You may not think so after we chat, Rachel." Henrietta Phillips's frosty gaze sought out the source of her apoplexy, lighting on the sheepish Meggie peeking around her mother's leg.

Atop the roof, Ben contemplated dropping the half-empty box of shingles on Miz Phillips's frizzy head to forestall her incrimination of Meggie, but he swiftly rejected that option. He wished with all his heart that Meggie had had the opportunity to confess her transgression before the stout battle-ax denounced her. He shook his head and pounded with a fury.

"Is something troubling you?" Rachel had to raise her voice an octave to make herself heard.

"In a word, it's that young'n of yours, Rachel," Miz Phillips shouted. "You know I'm not one to criticize, but Meggie's latest devilment leaves me no choice."

Rachel straightened to her full five feet five inches. "Maybe you should tell me exactly what my daughter has done to upset you so, Henrietta." Although her words were polite, her voice held a certain crisp intonation.

"She cropped off Dory's hair, that's what," the neighbor blurted. "She had no cause to do anything so vicious, neither. Just pure spite, that's what it was." She shook an accusing finger at the bug-eyed Meggie.

Rachel reached around and caught her daughter by the shoulder, hauling the red-faced tot to her side. Meggie could feel the tense bite of her mother's fingers as Rachel asked, "Is this true, Margaret Jane?"

"Well, it is and it isn't" was her nebulous reply. "I did snip Dory's hair. That part's true." She cracked her knuckles while confessing. "But Dory's been asking for it, Mama. She tries to rile me every chance she gets."

"Dory couldn't have done anything so bad as to deserve the shearing she got." Henrietta Phillips's face quivered with motherly indignation. "I ain't one to criticize, Rachel, you know I ain't, but Meggie's gotten wilder than a junkyard dog since Yancy's passin'. She needs to be taken in tow, that's what. She's becoming a downright menace. You should see my Dory. Why, I'm embarrassed for her to be seen in public. She looks like a plucked chicken."

It was an exaggeration, but not much of one. Rachel fought to keep her temper in check, but her grip on Meggie became viselike. "I'm sorry that Meggie would do such a thing and I'll gladly pay for Dory to have her hair tended to as soon as possible, but I'm not at all convinced that my daughter would resort to such meanness unless she were provoked." Before Henrietta could reply, Rachel set her straight. "I'm not one to be petty, Henrietta," she mocked, "but I've known for some time that Dory can be an agitator. Not so long ago, she tied Meggie to a tree and left her to swelter in the hot sun for hours while telling her it was part of an Indian rite and that brave warriors don't cry. And far be it from me to mention the countless times Dory has played malicious jokes on Meg-

107

gie, such as coaxing her to eat mud cakes or daring her to jump from the loft!"

Normally, Rachel wouldn't have dreamed of responding so tersely or pettily, but it had been a trying day and, unfortunately, Henrietta bore the brunt of the burgeoning stress. "I resent your telling me that my daughter is a menace to the community when your own is hardly a model of virtue," she went on. "Yancy had little to do with Meggie's rearing, and I'll thank you not to pass judgment or interfere in my private affairs. Now, was there anything else you wanted to discuss?" Her chin rose, and she stared down her pert nose at the aghast Henrietta.

"Well, I should've known you'd be resentful. You're not only a poor excuse for a mother, but you're as spiteful as that brat of yours."

"If you've said your piece, I'd appreciate it very much if you'd get your fat fanny off my property," Rachel snapped.

"With pleasure." Miz Phillips's 40-D bosom heaved as she strutted toward her station wagon. "By the way," she sputtered, jerking open the car door, "don't think you're foolin' anybody with your high and pious ways, Rachel Daniels. Just because you put in an appearance at church every Sunday don't mean we don't know what goes on around here Monday through Saturday. You ain't foolin' a soul." She cast a meaningful look upward in Ben's direction.

He took time out from his hammering to acknowledge the dirty-minded neighbor with a curt nod of his light-brown head.

Rachel trembled with rage as she watched the obnoxious busybody pull out of her drive. But no sooner had Henrietta Phillips's station wagon cleared the gate that

108

tears began to trickle down her crimson cheeks. Her hold on Meggie relaxed, and when she looked down at her daughter, the tot could see the telltale tracks of her mother's frustration.

"I'm sorry, Mama," she said sincerely.

Rachel was torn between two conflicting impulses—embracing her daughter so tightly that she might break, or spanking her so soundly that she might be scarred.

The screen door slammed as she dashed inside the house and scurried up the stairs to her room. It wasn't until she had locked the door and thrown herself onto the bed that she broke down and sobbed. Maybe she truly was a poor excuse for a mother. Maybe she had been too lax a disciplinarian and Meggie was taking advantage. Perhaps the child was too damned spirited for her own good. Tomorrow she would punish Meggie for her cruel prank. In addition to a spanking, there would be no snacks, no playmates, and no TV for two weeks. It had to be done. Meggie had to learn to accept the consequences of her actions.

She rolled onto her back and covered her eyes with an arm. Did Ben really think she was that easy? Did he think she'd trade her morals for a box of shingles? Why had she ever taken him on? What a poor choice of words!

Her fist pounded the feather mattress. Jesus! Please let it rain. She seconded Meggie's prayer, but for entirely different reasons, then groaned and pulled her knees up to her chest. It would all be for nothing, all her toil and turmoil, if the heavens didn't open up and the reviving rain pour down. Like the song, she wished that she could soon chant, "Lord, Lord, didn't it rain, didn't it rain." Spent and discouraged, she drifted off into a troubled sleep.

* * *

After the huffy departure of Miz Phillips, Ben had joined Meggie on the porch steps. She sat with her chin propped in her palms and her eyes downcast.

"Mama's really upset. She was crying, Ben. I never saw Mama cry before, not even when Daddy died."

He hugged her to him and kissed her forehead. "It's not you in particular, Meggie. It's everything in general." Suddenly he felt very inept. God only knew how much he wanted to reassure Meggie and comfort her mother.

"Am I bad, Ben?" Meggie wrapped her arms around his waist, clinging and demanding the reassurance he wanted so desperately to give.

He rocked her in his arms, crooning, "You're spirited, honey, just like your mama. Sometimes people mistake spirit for spite because they don't know how to deal with those whose values and expectations can't be compromised. You mustn't let them get you down. Instead, you should keep on tugging on the reins that would bind you, Meggie. No matter what, be as strong and special as your mother."

CHAPTER SEVEN

Sometime during the night, Rachel awakened with a start. She had been dreaming of a desolate desert where nothing but Gila monsters and cactus flourished. It was an endless sea of white, hot sand, and she was stranded without water or shade. Then suddenly, in the shimmering distance, she saw Ben, waving his arms and beckoning her toward a cool oasis. She started to run to him, but as she tried to cross the pumice wasteland, the sky turned bisque-colored, and it began to rain gritty sand. Drift upon drift impeded her progress, and before she could reach him, he and the oasis were buried under a giant dune. That's when she had lurched awake to find herself perspiring and gasping. It was a long moment before she could function rationally, and even then her skin still felt as though it bore traces of grit. An almost fanatical compulsion to bathe seized her.

She soaked in a hot tub for nearly an hour, then put on her favorite long white eyelet nightgown with blue ribbon lacing up the bodice, tied a dainty bow at the cleft of her cleavage, and crawled back into bed.

Dawn broke at precisely the same moment that a low ceiling of thunderheads moved over Mesquite Junction. There were no forewarning grumbles from the heavens, only a gentle pinging of raindrops on the roof. At first

Rachel didn't hear the glorious sound. But then her eyes blinked open, and she lay listening to the faint patter, trying to focus her mind. Was she dreaming again? Could it actually be rain that she heard rin-tin-tinning on the roof? She sat up alert in the bed. The wind gusted outside her open window, and on the sill a collection of beaded moisture had formed.

"Hallelujah!" she rejoiced, flinging back the sheet and darting from the bed. The ruffle at the hem of her gown flounced around her ankles as she trotted to the window and lifted the shade to look out at the farm. The wet, wet gloom was beautiful. The rows of cotton plants stretched in the showering mist to quench their thirst, the dry earth turned rich and moist before her very eyes, and the gentle rain shimmied down the barn's steepled roof and made welcomed puddles in the yard.

It wasn't a mirage like the oasis in her nightmare. She was wide awake, and it was really, really raining! She spread her arms wide and spun around and around in gleeful circles. As she danced a jig around the room, a thunderhead clapped high above the farmhouse, and the gentle shower heightened to a steady, soaking rain.

Unthinking and uncaring about anything else but the salvation of her crop, Rachel vaulted from the bedroom and scurried down the steps. Barefoot and lighthearted, she pattered past Ben's cubbyhole, through the kitchen, and out onto the back porch.

Ben awakened at the whack of the screen door. He sat up on the edge of the bed, yawned wide, and raked his hands through his hair. Jerking on his jeans, he dragged himself into the kitchen to pour himself a cup of coffee. He didn't hear or see the rain at first; he merely cussed when he discovered there was nothing perking. Typical, he thought to himself. No decent food, no ice for the cider, and no hot coffee. Rachel could be exasperating sometimes. Hell! He was being kind. Rachel was contrary a lot of the time.

He dumped the stale grounds into the trash, then staggered toward the sink to wash out the pot. It was then that he spied Rachel silhouetted against the gray morning light. He nearly dropped the pot when he realized she was doing a cross between a hula and a fandango in her nightie on the back porch. What in the world had come over her? Except for the night of their lovemaking, Rachel had worn only her work clothes or her Sunday best in his presence. He had never even seen her in a robe, let alone a filmy gown. Actually, he preferred her in the buff best, but he certainly wasn't about to complain. Fascinated, he watched as she hooked a hand around the porch railing and swung out into the rain.

Rain! Holy shit! Either he was having some kind of erotic fantasy, or it was sure as hell pouring down. Numbly, he deposited the coffeepot onto the counter and stepped out onto the porch.

Her swinging ceased, and her almond eyes were filled with warmth as she met his amused gaze. Then quite unexpectedly, she came to him, flung her arms around his neck, and kissed his cheek. If it weren't for the very real smell of her intoxicating perfume, he would have thought he was hallucinating.

Before he could react, she was skipping down the steps out into the yard and the rain like a wood nymph, chanting, "Feel it, Ben! It's wet, wet, wet! Dear God! We may just bring in this crop after all!" Throwing back her head, she opened her mouth and drank the raindrops, twirling in delirious loops. "Come enjoy it with me! We deserve to." The tears of happiness spilling down her face mingled with the healing rain. Her gown was becoming drenched and transparent, the wet material clinging to her slim and seductive figure. She was a barefoot goddess with a tinkling gypsy laugh, and he envied the rain that caressed her hair and trickled between her breasts.

Purposefully, he strode to where she stood, gathered her into his arms, and returned her kiss, only on the lips and in earnest. God only knew how much he wanted her again. A fire burned inside of him that not even a monsoon could smother.

He took her by storm, and she was powerless to resist him or her own desire. Though his embrace was crushing, it was also compelling. And though his kiss was near primitive, it was also addictive. She could feel the excited pounding of his heart and the hard rising of his passion. She sensed his urgency and could not deny the escalating need within herself. She moaned as his tongue stirred and savored her passion. She shuddered as he cupped and tenderly caressed her ripe breasts. And she went limp when he lifted her into his arms and carried her into the barn and laid her down upon a pallet of canvas that had once been Meggie's play tent.

"It isn't the rain that's a miracle, Rachel," he whispered hoarsely as he glided his hand beneath her gown and up her shapely leg. "It's you." He pressed his lips to her bare thigh, gliding them along the silk of her skin to a place just short of her panty line, just short of ecstasy.

She felt heady and wild. Ben was such an expert lover —forceful enough to be exciting and sensitive enough to be reassuring. A woman would have to be mad to refuse him. She'd missed him so terribly. A few kisses more couldn't hurt. Just to touch him and have him touch her. Why was it necessary to deprive herself?

She tangled her hands in his wet hair and guided his mouth to her own hungry one. Onehanded, he unlaced the bodice of her gown and spread wide the lapels, forsaking her lips and sampling her peaked nipples. Like petals opening to the sun, they blossomed in the warmth of his tender suckling.

He undid her gown further, exposing her sleek midriff and sprinkling kisses down to her stomach. She closed her eyes and drew a deep breath as he massaged the flat of her abdomen and then inched lower, lower still to where a pulsebeat that she had never known existed throbbed.

As if of their own volition, her fingers roamed his bronzed chest, then trailed to where a man longs to be touched. She had the knowledge and the sensitivity to arouse him as thoroughly as he had her. His breathing became labored, his face tensed, and he could no longer abide the few garments that separated him from her raw beauty.

"I want you so much, Rachel," he confessed, clutching the ruffled border of her gown and hiking it over her hips. Outside the barn, the rain continued to fall and the thunder rolled overhead. Suddenly, dampness permeated the musty refuge, and a harsh north wind banged shut the barn doors.

She shivered at his bold and efficient strip of her bikini underpants. Her mind focused on the unmistakable sound of his zipper, and the whole of her body froze. Too far. She'd gone too far! If they again consummated their passion, she knew she would fall hopelessly in love with him. She did not doubt that he wanted her as desperately as she wanted him. He was a man of strong feelings—but strong didn't necessarily mean enduring. A storm surge could be strong at the onset and then dwindle and recede. God help her, she must not forget that Ben had the same disastrous potential as a cyclone—appearing out of nowhere, stirring everything up, and moving on once the damage was done.

Abruptly, she covered herself, sat up, and placed a negating hand on Ben's arm. She hadn't the courage to look at him, for she knew the stun she would encounter in his eyes. "I can't, Ben." Her denial sounded feeble and hollow. She drew up her legs, locked her arms around them, and cradled her forehead on her knees. Then, clearing her throat, she offered an excuse for her baffling behavior. "I can't risk letting myself care for you. And I will, sure as hell I will, if we keep this up."

He bounded to his feet and zipped up his jeans. She dared to lift her head and engage his flashing eyes. "Answer me something, Rachel. What in the hell were the last thirty minutes about? Am I supposed to believe that that was an expression of indifference?"

She fumbled for an answer while groping for her frilly bikini pants. "You ought to know by now that I tend to cling to whatever I love. It's not necessarily a good trait, but it's how I am. Nothing cleaves to a rolling stone. And that's what you are, Ben Eaton." Self-consciously, she wriggled into her panties, then tripped on the hem of her nightie as she tried to stand, clumsily staggering into his inflexible figure.

His hands gripped the soft flesh of her shoulders, and he shook her so hard that her head bobbed. "You're not only peculiar, but infuriating, Rachel Daniels. For the life of me, I don't know what attracts me to you." He released her so suddenly that she stumbled backward a step.

"Try to understand, dammit! In a month or so, you'll be gone from here. I don't want to miss or grieve for you. I've got a farm to run, a future to make for Meggie. It'll take all of me to do that. I can't afford the part of myself

116

that you'd take with you when you leave." She hugged her chest to stave off the impaling look in his eyes.

Jesus! How he wanted to confess his desire to stay on with her, how he longed to profess his love for her! Yet something inside him couldn't differentiate between old rejections and the affront his masculine pride had suffered just moments before. He analyzed her revealing choice of words: "Can't risk letting myself *care* for you"; "don't want to *miss* or *grieve* for you." Not once had she mentioned love. One could care for an object or a pet; one could miss an indulgent habit; one could grieve for a lost opportunity or pleasure. In the absence of love, one could fill the void with any or all of the poor substitutes. Which category did he fall into? he wondered. His own insecurity searched for protection for his strong feelings and vulnerabilities.

"Fine, just fine," he spat, his jaw flexing as he narrowed the space between them. "Now that I know exactly where things stand between us, I'll be sure to keep my distance, ma'am. I sure as hell don't want to complicate your orderly life." He cast her a final scathing glance, then stomped out of the barn and started across the yard.

She traipsed after him, hiking her gown and skirting the puddles. "There's no sense in you being angry with me. I'm just trying to be honest. Will you please wait? Let's discuss this like two civil adults." She slipped and slid in the mud, her wet ringlets bobbing, her gown saturated.

He turned on her so fast, she nearly collided with him again.

"You don't know what the hell you want, Rachel," he told her angrily. "You can't have it both ways. The only

117

commitment you're willing to make is to this stinking farm. Well, so be it, but don't ask me to like it."

"I have no choice. It's the way it has to be. I'm not free like you to do whatever I please."

He gazed off at the revitalized fields, oblivious to the pelting rain, aware only of her rejection. "What do you want me to say, Rachel? That I understand and it doesn't matter? That I'll finish out the season regardless of the friction between us?"

"It would ease my mind immensely," she admitted in a low voice.

He glared at her. "I'll stick it out on one condition."

"Which is?" She could hardly breathe, and the mud felt like quicksand beneath her feet.

"That whatever I do on my personal time is none of your affair. I don't intend to hibernate on this farm until harvest." He paused. "Unlike you, I have other needs." His wounded ego demanded satisfaction.

She knew what he was implying, and it made her sick with jealousy. "I've never made you feel you couldn't pursue external interests," she said defensively.

"Oh, yes, you have," he rebutted, turning his back on her and taking shelter in the house.

Dejectedly, she trudged to the porch and flopped upon the swing. Her gaze drifted over her fields, taking some solace in the security of her land. If Ben Eaton thought she would crumble at the prospect of him socializing with the likes of Desiree Sayer, he was sadly mistaken. Hadn't that been her point entirely? She was determined to maintain her objectivity so as not to fall fatally in love with him.

She swayed back and forth in the swing, blocking from her mind the distasteful thought of Ben with another woman. If she refused to seriously reflect upon his stipulation, then surely she could deny him space in her heart.

"Mornin', Mama," Meggie greeted, rubbing her sleepy eyes and climbing up into the swing beside her mother. "Are you feeling better today?"

Nestling both the child and her teddy bear close, Rachel mustered a smile. "Much better, honey," she assured her with a kiss atop the head.

"Ben's talking to himself in the bathroom again." Margaret Jane nestled against her mother's comfy bosom.

Rachel could only imagine the content of his ranting.

"What's does *inhibited tease* mean?"

"It's not a flattering term" was all her mother could answer, silently fuming. Inhibited tease, indeed!

"Is *hard-ass woman* not flattering, either?" Meggie's head bumped against the back of the porch swing at her mother's abrupt exit.

Rachel strutted posthaste to the bathroom and pounded on the door. She'd show him a hard-ass woman! "I'll thank you to keep your opinions to yourself, Ben Eaton, and don't you dare use all the hot water!"

By the time he answered, Rachel had huffed upstairs. Only Meggie stood guard in the hall, looking suspiciously innocent.

"What the heck is the matter with her now?" Ben barked.

Meggie merely shrugged, offering a yawn and an "I dunno" before stuffing a doughnut into her mouth.

CHAPTER EIGHT

Although it rained for several days, by the time the Sunday picnic date with Jonas rolled around, the ground was dry and the sun was shining brightly.

During the preceding week the new semester had begun, and Meggie had joined the ranks of first graders having to adjust to a full day of attendance at school. This meant that Rachel and Ben had to try to deal with each other without her buffering presence. Under the circumstances it wasn't easy. So to compensate, they thrust themselves into work and made a supreme effort not to violate the tenuous truce between them.

As he'd vowed, Ben kept a respectful distance, for the most part communicating only when it was essential and then only generally. He seldom even looked her direction. If some unavoidable duty required him to come into close contact with her, he immediately retreated once the task was done. He rarely addressed her as Rachel anymore, but substituted a curt "no, ma'am" or formal "yes, Miz Daniels" whenever the occasion dictated that he speak to her at all. And although his indifferent manner irritated her to no end, she masked her irritation and responded with disinterest. They both knew they'd reached an impasse in their relationship.

Somehow they'd each made it through the rest of the

week without giving an inch or gaining an advantage. Saturday passed with only one awkward incident to mark it—the baking of the chocolate fudge cake she had promised to Jonas McMurtry for Sunday's picnic. When Ben came through the kitchen to wash up for dinner, he spotted the dessert sitting on the table and paused.

"Don't it look good?"

His eyes traveled to Margaret Jane, who sat on the kitchen counter licking the icing out of a bowl. "Mama says we can't have any tonight. It's for the picnic tomorrow. But she's sure some'll be left over, and we can have a piece later if we want." She sucked the last bit of icing from off her finger.

"That's awfully generous of her," he muttered, fighting a powerful impulse to spit at the fudge masterpiece.

Rachel cleared her throat to let him know she was in the pantry and could hear his snide remarks.

He ignored her, shooting Meggie a devilish wink before proceeding down the hall. When he returned, the offensive cake had been taken out of sight, and Rachel did not refer to it or to his sarcastic crack throughout the entire evening.

Yet when McMurtry arrived the next day to claim Rachel and the promised Sunday afternoon treat, Ben got testy all over again. It really galled him that Rachel would lavish such a favor on her former beau when she couldn't even so much as flip a pancake for him. He hoped she and McMurtry both contracted food poisoning.

Looking sexy and smelling sweeter than a field of wild flowers, Rachel handed Jonas the plastic cake carrier and climbed into his Jeep. "You're to do as Ben says," she told Meggie.

Sitting on the porch steps with her toes turned in, her

elbows propped upon her scraped knees, and her pudgy cheeks pressed between her palms, Meggie nodded dismally, then wrinkled up her nose at Jonas when she was sure he wasn't looking. No sooner had he put the Jeep into reverse that she went to find Ben. She found him in the barn muttering to himself again as he buffed a brush across his battered boots.

"Whatcha doing in here?" she asked, plopping herself beside him.

"Practicing biofeedback," he growled.

"Is it hard?" She hadn't the faintest notion of what he was talking about.

"Sometimes." About now, his blood pressure had to be nearing stroke level.

Meggie fidgeted. "Got anything special you want to do today?"

Getting staggeringly drunk and letting Meggie baby-sit him were high on his list at the moment. "Do you?" he countered, positive she'd have at least a dozen suggestions as to how they might entertain themselves. He knew the child well enough to realize that she planned to take full advantage of his novice guardianship.

"Well," she mulled, as if she hadn't already plotted a mischievous caper, "we could go fishin'."

The boot he was buffing dropped from his hand. "Forget it, Meggie." His tone implied that the point was non-negotiable.

Meggie pretended not to notice. "Why can't we? It's a free country. Jonas McMurtry don't own the pond."

Ben refused to debate it.

Meggie was not about to drop the idea. "Aren't you bored? I sure am. Cory Thompson told me at school that the fish were practically jumping into his net. I got some worms, and I'll be good as gold. Quiet as a mouse. Mama

122

and Jonas won't even know we're there. I swear. Scout's honor." She held up three fingers in a solemn pledge.

Ben had to laugh at her persistence. "You're not old enough to be a Scout," he reminded her.

She looked up at him with big puppy-dog eyes. "But I'll soon be. And it counts just the same."

He knew it was a ridiculous idea, but the chance to nix McMurtry's wooing ritual was too tempting. He set aside the boots and scrutinized her. "You should definitely go into politics when you grow up." The grudging smile that broke on his face told her she had succeeded in convincing him.

"Does that mean we can go to the pond?" Triumphant dimples appeared as she crooked her head to peer up at him.

"Load the gear into the pickup." He said, giving her curls a playful ruff.

"I already did." At the accusing crook of his brow, she quickly added, "I figured it'd save time just in case you said yes."

He shook his head, almost feeling an empathy for Jonas McMurtry's impending plight.

Obviously, Meggie's definition of *good as gold* and *quiet as a mouse* differed greatly from the usual meaning of those words. No sooner had she and Ben arrived at the pond than she trotted over to where her mother and Jonas were picnicking beneath a tree and announced herself.

"What are you doing here, Margaret Jane?" Rachel's gaze darted to Ben, who was baiting the cane poles on the opposite bank of the pond.

Jonas managed to maintain a tight-lipped smile, but he was more than mildly annoyed.

123

"Fishin' " was the tot's spare reply.

"Have you forgotten that you're being punished still, missy? Being grounded means just that—you are not to venture off the farm."

Meggie had prepared a legitimate excuse. "I can't help it if Ben was just bustin' to go fishin'. I told him I wasn't allowed, but he said he shouldn't leave me all alone. I won't fish or have any fun if you don't want me to." Her self-sacrificing overture was almost believable.

Rachel sighed, then reluctantly relented. "Since you're here, I suppose you might as well go ahead and fish." She definitely planned to have a private word with Ben Eaton. His sudden yen to visit the pond was most suspicious and was more than likely malicious. "Now run along, Meggie. Mr. McMurtry and I would like to picnic in peace."

She truly hoped Meggie would occupy herself with fishing but, knowing her flighty nature, she highly doubted it. "I'm sorry about the extra company, Jonas," she apologized as she spread the basket of goodies onto the blanket. "Now, what was it you were saying?"

He scooted closer and took a container of potato salad from her hand. "I was recalling those pleasant evenings when we used to come here to the pond and think about our future. It seems like just yesterday."

She smiled wistfully. "You were so excited about escaping from Mesquite Junction and attending college up north. I'll never forget how impressed I was at your determination to better yourself."

"Yeah, I had a lot of grand ideas then. I thought that I would be president of General Motors before my thirtieth birthday, or at the very least a first-draft choice and then a celebrated running back in the NFL. Things didn't work out as I'd expected. Instead, I ended up not even

124

making first string and eventually taking over the family business right back here in Lubbock County." His eyes downcast, he watched a steady stream of industrious ants carry off breadcrumbs.

Rachel was moved by the disappointment in his voice. "Not very much turned out the way any of us had thought. Unlike you, I didn't harbor any grand notions, but I hoped for an easier life."

"If we had ended up together like we should've, your life would have been very different." He glanced up at the exact same instant that her own almond gaze drifted to her daughter across the pond. He hated himself for feeling jealous of a child, and yet he secretly resented the devotion Rachel gave to Meggie. "Had things turned out the way we once planned, you would have been my wife, not Yancy's."

She shrugged. "We were just kids when we talked of marrying, Jonas. We had no way of knowing the different courses our lives would take. It was naïve of us to think that time and distance wouldn't test our feelings for one another."

"It was all my fault," he lamented. "I should've realized that the old-fashioned girl I left waiting back home was ten times a better woman than the campus flirts. But I started dating Lorraine because she was wild and had no compunction about jumping into the sack at the slightest incentive. She was a novelty, a scarlet rose, so different from the shy violets I was accustomed to. The sheets weren't even cold from our fooling around when she was already telling her folks and our friends that we were practically engaged. I'm not making excuses for myself, but I swear I just didn't know how to bow out. What a damned fool I was. Lorraine didn't care for me any more than I did for her. Her intent all along was to snare a potential money-maker."

Rachel sat utterly dumbfounded. She'd never guessed the real reason for Jonas's defection. "Why are you telling me this now, Jonas, when you never felt the need to explain yourself at the time?"

"Because it matters, Rachel. I made concessions and mistakes that I regret. I want you to know—"

"Whaddya think, Mama? Is it a keeper?" Meggie dangled a guppie-size catch between them.

Jonas gritted his teeth to keep from snapping, "Hell, no! Throw it back into the pond and yourself after it!"

Rachel expressed herself much more kindly. "It's not a keeper, honey. I should think Ben would be a better judge than I am. Check with him next time, won't you?"

"Okay," Meggie said a little hesitantly. "But he's awfully busy talkin' to Miz Sayer, and it isn't polite to interrupt."

Jonas curbed an impulse to remind the pesty kid that she certainly hadn't hesitated to interrupt him.

At the mention of Desiree, Rachel shaded her eyes and scanned the pond's bank. Sure enough, there she sat in a lawn chair beside Ben, looking like a Delta belle in organza ruffles and a wide-brimmed straw hat. No doubt she was drawling all over herself!

"Well, next time get Ben's opinion. He won't mind, I'm sure." Patting the tot on the fanny, she sent her to do her dirty work.

"Now, where were we?" she asked Jonas, giving him only her halfhearted attention.

He sensed her distraction and wondered if it was entirely due to Meggie's badgering. "All I was trying to say was that if I had to do it all over again, I wouldn't make the same mistake. You and I were very good together once, Rachel. I know you loved Yancy, but—"

"Yes, yes, I did," she confirmed, unable to refrain from glancing in Ben's direction at the sound of Desiree's lilting laughter.

"But he's gone and, well, uh"—expressing himself was not going nearly as well in practice as it had in theory—"I'm free now."

"I'm well aware of that," she responded vaguely, torn between Jonas's ramblings and Desiree's outrageous exposure of her ample bosom to Ben as she bent to assist him with the bait bucket.

Jonas leaned in front of Rachel, blocking her view and tipping her chin with a fingertip. "You're breaking your back trying to make that damned farm work, Rachel. We both know Yancy's to blame for your problems, and it's a damned shame. It's hard for me to stand by and watch you struggle. I care about you. I want to—"

Another fish shimmied on a string between them. "It's tangled on the hook! I can't get it off," Meggie complained.

At that moment Jonas wanted to string Meggie up. Couldn't the brat do anything for herself?

"Here, let me see it," Rachel patiently offered, glad that Jonas had not had the chance to recite the speech she was sure he had prepared.

Meggie flopped onto the blanket, flashing Jonas a toothy grin. "So are you having a swell time?"

"Yeah, swell," he pouted, reaching for a chicken leg and biting into it with a gnash of his teeth.

Margaret Jane looked covetously at the fudge cake beneath the plastic cover. "Your cake sure looks fine, Mama," she praised. "I bet it tastes even better."

Rachel continued trying to work the hook free. "I have

suspicions about why you are being so complimentary, Meggie, and it won't work."

Her daughter immediately became indignant at the suggestion. "I don't want any cake! But Ben might, 'specially since today is his birthday 'n all."

The hook broke loose at Rachel's tug. She slanted a skeptical look at Margaret Jane and handed her the fish and cane pole. "If you're concocting some fictitious birthday just to wheedle some cake, I'm going to be very upset with you, missy," she warned.

Although Meggie's fibbing heart missed a beat, she decided she was in too deep to change her story. Besides, her mouth was watering to sample the treat. "I heard him tell Miz Sayer," she declared convincingly.

Rachel felt sick at the thought of slighting Ben on his birthday. After all, he had no one with whom to celebrate, except Desiree, of course, whom she was certain would like nothing better than to make a present of herself to him. She looked entreatingly at Jonas, who wanted nothing more than to buy the troublesome hired hand a one-way ticket out of town in honor of the occasion.

He read her mind. "Sure, why not? Go ahead and invite Ben and Desiree to join us," he grudgingly conceded aloud and wondered to himself how a six-year-old had managed to undermine months of courtship in one afternoon.

It hadn't occurred to Rachel to invite Desiree, but it was impossible to exclude her without looking petty. "Go ask them if they would care to share some cake with us, Meggie," she instructed.

The words had barely crossed her lips when Meggie dashed off to deliver the unexpected invitation. The tricky part would be to break the news of his premature birthday to Ben without Miz Sayer hearing. Once on the opposite bank, Meggie pardoned herself to Miz Sayer and then tugged Ben aside.

"Mama wants to know if you and Miz Sayer would care to join she and Jonas for cake," she panted.

Needless to say, Ben was speechless.

"But there's somethin' you ought to know before you accept." Meggie didn't know quite how to explain her deviousness. Aware that both her mother and Miz Sayer were watching, she decided to coach Ben so as not to give herself away. "What I'm gonna say might make you mad, but if you look like a cloud set on your face, I'm gonna be in a pile of trouble. So try to act natural, will ya?"

Ben had a sinking feeling in the pit of his stomach. "Just tell me what you've done," he prompted.

"I told Mama it was your birthday so she would share the cake," she blurted in one breath.

"Tell me you didn't," he pleaded.

"I just told you I did," she whispered. "I know I shouldn't have. It just sorta popped out. Besides, your birthday's soon, ain't it?"

"Not even close."

"Well, for my sake, could you pretend it's today?" She crossed her fingers and prayed.

Ben raked his hair back from his forehead and cursed beneath his breath.

"Mama's getting antsy, Ben. You just gotta do it, or else I'm gonna be grounded until I'm as old as Annie Baird."

Her pathetic expression reminded him of a frightened rabbit caught in a trap. "Okay, Meggie. I'll go along with this, but only if you give me your solemn word that you'll swallow your tongue before you tell such a blatant lie ever again. Next time, you won't get off so easy."

"I promise. Scout's honor." Once more, she held up three fingers in a pledge. Considering how soon she'd forgotten her earlier oath, he was not reassured.

"Come on." He caught her none too gently by the neck and marched her toward Desiree. "I suppose we should inform Miz Sayer that I'm a year older today before we make it a foursome for cake. Dammit, Meggie! This is a hell of a mess you've gotten us into."

"I know," she agreed, silently thanking the Almighty for making Ben so understanding.

Meggie sat against a tree trunk wolfing down the fudge cake and watching the adults behave like children.

Jonas was peeved and took issue with Ben every chance he got. No matter what the subject was, he expressed an opposing view. Ben was hardly in the mood to put up with Jonas's bull, and he kept cramming cake into his mouth to keep from saying something crude in the ladies' presence.

Miz Sayer kept gushing that Ben looked more like twenty-five than thirty-five and that she had a strawberry shortcake recipe that simply *melted* in a person's mouth and that her ex-husband had never appreciated her fine baking ability, let alone the more personal touches at which she was so adept.

Rachel's smile looked as if it were plastered onto her face, and she kept contradicting Miz Sayer about insignificant details, such as that it could not have been her late husband Yancy who had fixed her plumbing two years ago August, for he would've mentioned it if he had.

"Well, I suppose I could be mistaken," Miz Sayer crawfished. "By the way, Ben, would you be interested in doing a few odd chores for me?" Noting Rachel's slam of the picnic basket lid, she wisely amended, "That is to say,

130

only if you're willing and if Rachel can spare you, of course."

"Mr. Eaton is not my personal property, Desiree. You talk as if he were a lackey or something. He can work at whatever and for whomever he pleases anytime the notion strikes him." Rachel had set the record straight, and while she was at it, just for good measure, she primped the skirt of her taupe sundress.

Vying for a fair share of the attention, Jonas passed his plate to Rachel for seconds. She obliged with a coquettish smile, showing Desiree that she didn't have a monopoly on eligible men.

Ben thanked his boss for being so thoughtful as to commemorate his birthday, but he declined a second piece in a show of willpower. The look that passed between them was anything but PG-rated, and the hostility they emitted was about as subtle as fireworks on the fourth of July.

"Since I don't need Miz Daniels's permission, I'll be glad to stop by and take care of any small problems you may have."

"Well, aren't you obliging!" Desiree cooed. "I don't suppose you'd consider my lack of an escort to the Harvest Social a small problem, would you?"

Meggie wondered if perhaps Miz Sayer had dust in her eyes, the way she kept blinking them.

"That's not small, Desiree," Ben drawled thoughtfully, which made Rachel believe he was smart enough not to be taken in by the divorcee's magnolia charm. "It's a major oversight by the men around here." He stated the compliment as if it were a fact. "I'd be more than willing to take you."

"How sweet," she hummed demurely, casting Rachel a haughty smirk.

Meggie was unsure if it was the three helpings of fudge cake or Miz Sayer's syrup that was making her stomach queasy.

"Mama, I don't feel so good," she interjected.

"What is it, honey?" Out of habit, Rachel felt her forehead.

"I dunno. My tummy sorta hurts, and I don't think I want any more cake." Meggie looked at Ben. He knew what she was thinking—that maybe God was punishing her for having told a bare-faced lie.

"Too much fishing in the hot sun," he assured her with a wink.

"We need to take her home, Jonas." Rachel began to pack up.

It figured, Jonas thought, lending a hand. Meggie was going to see to it that he didn't even get a farewell peck. Well, things would change once he took charge. Yancy's offspring would soon learn that her mother was not her private domain.

"I'll be along shortly," Ben whispered to Meggie while he piggybacked her to the Jeep. Her arms tightened around his neck.

"Happy birthday, Ben," she wished him, feeling strangely threatened and glad he was near.

CHAPTER NINE

During the following days the frosty standoff between Rachel and Ben thawed a bit. Although they did not recapture the warmth that had once been, they were at least cordial to one another. The two ties that bound them—Meggie and the cotton crop—forced the willful woman and the disillusioned man to share both the good and bad of a common goal. Regardless of the lost intimacy, their mutual devotion forged their spirits as surely as molten carbon and iron create steel. They were united in their objective—to insure Meggie's future happiness and security by bringing in a bumper cotton crop this season.

It was the final week of September—only hours away from the Harvest Social and a few weeks away from ginning the cotton. Together they inspected the fields at sunset, then stood and reflected on the fruits of their labor.

"Have you noticed that farmland has a smell all its own?" She breathed deeply, savoring the earthy essence.

"Manure and sweat usually do." An easy grin spread across his tanned face.

"I suppose so." She laughed. "But where is the character in sterile skyscrapers and concrete mazes? I wouldn't trade one minute of this hardship for living in a congested city where the air is polluted and the pace is stifling."

He recalled the hectic pressures of Dallas and felt far removed from the shallowness of his prior existence. He identified more now with the wide open spaces of the plains and with the goodness of these folk who understood the value of such intangible assets as peace and trust and satisfaction. "I understand why you've fought so hard to hang on, Rachel. Mesquite Junction isn't just a speck on a map; it's a way of life. Meggie shouldn't be deprived of the contentment you've known. The solidity of this will reinforce her always."

"You sound as if you've grown fond of the plains." She admired his profile and marveled at how very handsome he was. Like this quiet and durable land, there was an underlying strength about him. Occasionally, if you looked closely, you could perceive smoldering defiance in his hazel eyes. He was a committed man, maybe not to God, but to himself and to whatever particular cause he chose to undertake.

"I have" was all he answered. It was because of her that he'd become attached to the land. Farming wasn't particularly exciting work; it was she who made it special. Somehow she managed to generate enthusiasm about nature's never-ending cycle and at the same time to preserve tradition and solid values. Yes, the widow possessed a gift for nurturing what was born anew each season, and yet she also revered what was enduring.

Their eyes met, and in that unguarded moment the deep affection they felt for one another could not be denied. The tender look they exchanged was one of regret and a silent apology for whatever pain they had caused each other in the name of pride. Later, they would each wonder who had found the strength to look away first.

"I suppose we should be heading back to the house. Desiree would never forgive me if you were late picking her up for the dance tonight. It's the social event of the year." Somehow she managed to sound casual about his date with the divorcee, but her heart ached at the thought of having to witness his attentiveness to another. During the past few weeks, each time he had made a trip out to Desiree's to take care of some petty emergency, she had died a little inside imagining what was transpiring between the two of them. Desiree was doing her damnedest to monopolize his every free moment. Rachel was positive that the sultry brunette was also doing her utmost to seduce him.

"I suppose we should." He tried to appear enthusiastic about the dance, but it was difficult, especially knowing he would have to witness Jonas McMurtry's systematic pursuit of Rachel. The man acted as if it were a foregone conclusion that she would become the next first lady of his seed and supply store. Even Meggie sensed his intent and felt threatened by it. "You and Jonas are going, aren't you?" At a leisurely pace they strolled back toward the house.

"Yes, of course."

He could have done without that matter-of-fact "of course." "What arrangements are you making for Meggie?"

Did she detect a hint of disapproval in his tone, or was she imagining it because she felt guilty about excluding her daughter from the festivities? "I've hired a sitter for the evening. I thought about bringing her along, but Jonas thought she'd be bored at such a grownup affair."

Ben bet that McMurtry's phony concern was for his own, not Meggie's, interests. "A sitter is probably less risky than another stint at the Phillips place."

135

"Henrietta hasn't spoken a word to me since our run-in over the girls. Not that I care," she added, kicking a soccer ball out of her path. "After what she said about Meggie and the insinuations about us, I wouldn't spit on the woman if she were on fire."

Ben couldn't help but laugh aloud at her spunky retort. "I didn't think a good Christian woman like yourself would hold such a grudge." He paused at the bottom of the porch steps, admiring the sway of her hips as she climbed up ahead of him.

She turned and slanted him a sizing look. "Do me or mine wrong sometime, and you'll see just how hard a grudge I can hold. If you'd read the Old Testament, you'd find many examples of God smiting his enemies."

He conceded the point with a blasphemous "Praise the Lord and pass the ammunition, eh?" at which she rolled her eyes and strutted into the house.

He shrugged and checked his watch. Even though the celebration tonight at the church recreation hall was to the folks in Mesquite Junction as big an affair as Mardi Gras was to the revelers in New Orleans, he would just as soon forgo all the fuss. He was hardly in the mood to celebrate the end of a growing season and the beginning of a harvest. The bargain he and Rachel had struck would soon be fulfilled. It saddened him to think of the moment when she'd pay him his back wages and expect him to make an exit. Leaving this serene farm and such a fine woman would be difficult.

He wasn't the same man who had first hired on with the widow. He, as well as the cotton crop, had matured through the growing season. The embittered man who had had no interest in life had come to realize how sweet and very precious a child's laughter was and how tender and restoring a farm woman's touch could be. Rachel and Meggie's zest for life was contagious. They were like a curative that revitalized an anemic soul.

Deep in his heart Ben knew that no matter how far he might travel, he would carry the memory of Rachel and Meggie wherever he went. He'd remember them always and would yearn to relive the memorable season when he had aided a widow in distress. Meggie he had adored upon first sight; Rachel had won his heart much more gradually but every bit as surely. Throughout the long, hot summer, he had fallen in love with her—head over heels, crazy in love with her.

He would've preferred not to have. He had tried his damnedest to convince himself that she had no claim on him, that he could erase her memory with a fling and never look back when it came time to hitch a ride out of Mesquite Junction. Unfortunately, that time was nearly at hand—only weeks away. Summer had become autumn, and he had become the widow's devoted admirer. There was a world beyond the Daniels farm gates, he knew. Yet somehow, the rest of the world lacked the appeal it had once held. He hadn't given a thought to where he would go next, whether to travel north, east, south, or west. It mattered little, for Rachel would not be at the end of his journey. Nor did it make much difference to him how he'd sustain himself in the dismal months ahead. Only Rachel made a difference, because only Rachel had the ability to breathe spirit back into his disillusioned soul.

Shaking his head, he sat on the steps and covered his face with his hands, thinking what a damned fool he'd been to believe that Desiree Sayer, with all her experience and willingness, could compete with Rachel. When the hot-blooded divorcee had guilefully maneuvered herself onto his lap and whispered an explicit solicitation into his ear, he hadn't gone through with it. Desiree had quickly realized the reason why.

"It's Rachel, isn't it?" she'd guessed, sliding from his lap with a disgusted sigh.

He neither confirmed or denied her suspicion as he stood and collected his Stetson from the hall hat rack.

"I don't mind soothin' a wounded ego, honey. But I'm not a'tall thrilled about being rejected before I even have the chance. Stay awhile longer. I'm an expert at making a man feel good."

"I'm sure you are, Desiree, but . . ." He had tried to salvage both of their dignities.

"But what? Don't tell me you've actually fallen for that sexless mule? Why, she couldn't even satisfy her own husband," she'd scoffed. "He didn't come all the way out here to fix my leaky plumbing just to be neighborly. Yancy had no complaints, and neither will you." Artfully, she arranged herself on the couch so that the slinky robe she wore parted provocatively, just enough to expose an ample section of thigh. With a lazy crook of her finger, she motioned for him to return to her arms.

It was all he could do not to display the revulsion he felt. "I'm not Yancy, Desiree. Hard as it may be for you to believe, I prefer a woman who's a bit more subdued. I'm sorry I led you to think otherwise. Let's just leave it at that, okay?"

"And I suppose you're going to renege on taking me to the Harvest Social, too?" she'd pouted.

"I said I'd take you, and I will. But do us both a favor and don't phone with any more half-baked excuses for me to drop by. I don't need the extra few bucks, and the fringe benefits don't appeal to me."

"Don't worry, I won't. There are plenty of eager men who will be more than happy to be at my beck and call.

138

Just be sure you don't stand me up next Saturday night, or I might be tempted to tell the whole damned county that you're willing to settle for my ex-lover's leftovers." She had seconded the threat with a vindictive smile.

"I'll bet you and Yancy were a hell of a match. By the way, did you know that you weren't his only indiscretion? Maybe you ought to have a chat with a barmaid by the name of Marybeth Waylon. The two of you could have a swell time comparing notes." And with that he had left the astounded Desiree to rant and curse alone.

As much as Ben hated the thought of subjecting himself to Desiree's bitchiness all evening, he didn't feel as if he had a choice. It was better to placate the wily brunette than to run the risk of her actually carrying out her threat. Her nasty gossip would devastate Rachel. Yancy had given her enough trouble while he lived. The last thing she needed was to have to endure the humiliation of hearing about his infidelities a year and a half after his death.

Feeling more like he was attending a wake than a celebration, Ben hauled himself to his feet and squared his broad shoulders. By tomorrow the Harvest Social would be history. He only hoped that when the townsfolk recalled this year's celebration, not a hint of smut would surface to undermine Rachel's confidence.

Meggie's compliment, "You look just like an angel," was apropos. Rachel did look divine in the gauzy white linen dress she had bought especially for the dance, and her blond curls, which were piled high atop her head and fastened with ivory combs, shimmered in the moonlight.

Only once before had Ben seen anything as fragile and lovely—a china doll that his mother kept high on the shelf of a curio cabinet in the upstairs hall, a gift from his father that he'd brought back from Switzerland. As a young boy, he had often stood before the treasure and admired its perfection. His mother had said the doll was priceless, something to be cherished. Now, at this awe-struck moment, that was his thought about Rachel. He doubted that even a master craftsman could have dupli-cated the delicacy he beheld.

"Are you having a nice time, Ben?" she asked him at the dance, replenishing her plastic cup with another dip-perful of punch.

His gaze swept the crowd of dancers, spying Desiree in the arms of a toothpick-slim farmer. Fred Astaire he was not. The clodhopper stepped on her toes and she stum-bled backward, rear-ending the goosey Reverend Log-gins, who pancaked himself against his partner Henrietta Phillips's size 40-D's. "Actually, I'm enjoying myself im-mensely at the moment," he chuckled.

Rachel misinterpreted the gleam in his eye as he watched Desiree Sayer two-step by. "Desiree is always a popular partner at these shindigs. You'll probably have to cut in if you want to dance with your date."

"She doesn't seem to miss me much" was all he said, dreading the thought of placing himself in the divorcee's clutches.

She sipped the punch, wishing Ben would ask her to dance while Jonas was conversing with a few of his dis-satisfied customers in a corner.

"Would you care to?" he offered, nodding toward the dance floor.

Thinking he had read her mind, she all but strangled on the punch. "If you're sure Desiree wouldn't mind."

Wordlessly, he took the cup from her hand and set it on the table, then led her toward the twirling couples.

140

When he took her in his arms, an imperceptible shiver ran over her. She kept her eyes demurely downcast, heedless of the music, yet moving in perfect sync with him.

It took every ounce of his self-control not to forge her to him. He wanted so much to experience the soft give of her body, to bask in the warmth of her womanliness one last time. Instead, he appeased himself with a featherlight brush of his lips against her satin hair. He dared not risk handling her recklessly lest their tenuous truce be broken like his mother's delicate Swiss doll.

As a lad, the temptation had been too great to resist, and he'd climbed to the top shelf of the curio cabinet to examine the intriguing doll more closely. He'd lost his footing, and to his horror, the cabinet had toppled like a felled tree. All of the rare and cherished heirlooms had shattered on impact with the terrazzo floor. The beautiful china doll had been crushed, and the spanking he'd received had not hurt nearly as much as his guilt at having destroyed something so wondrously beautiful. Not until Rachel had he thought again about the regrettable incident.

"My, but you're preoccupied. Judging from the faraway look in your eyes, you must be at least a thousand miles from here." She mustered a smile, though in her heart she worried that he was thinking of his future, that he was growing impatient to leave the farm and drift to parts unknown.

"More like thirty years away. I was remembering a childhood calamity," he murmured, embracing her closer to avoid a collision with Desiree and her clumsy partner.

The divorcee flashed him a murderous look from over the farmer's bony shoulder. He reciprocated with a tight grin.

"I'll bet you were a stinker as a kid," Rachel was saying, unaware of the daggers being aimed at her back.

"Spirited is how my mother used to phrase it," he corrected. "She preferred not to acknowledge my rebellious nature. If I misbehaved, she blamed it on the wildcatting genes I inherited from my father's side of the family."

Rachel couldn't help but note the cynicism in his voice. "Your family's rejection still bothers you very much, doesn't it?"

The empathy he saw in her soft eyes made him desperately want to share the great, sometimes engulfing need within him to reach out. "Sometimes, Rachel," he admitted. "Even if the reasons are valid, it doesn't lessen the sting of the rejection."

She glanced away, cradling her cheek against his shoulder and murmuring, "I know, Ben. If only—"

The music stopped, keeping her from sharing the wish.

"If only what, Rachel?" he urged.

At that critical instant, Jonas materialized out of nowhere to request a private word with her. Helplessly, Ben watched him lead her to a gazebo a discreet distance away. Damn, but he had wanted to hear what she'd been on the verge of expressing! He knew in his soul that she cared for him, but the situation between them was becoming more impossible each moment. Either she had to choose to commit, or he would have to reconcile his feelings for her. Under no circumstances would he try to influence her decision; only a fool would accept a one-sided love.

"Did the widow desert you, sugar?" Desiree hummed, linking her arm through his. "I told you she hadn't hormones enough to appreciate a real man. Well, never you mind, honey. If you're hot and bothered, we can skinny-dip down at the pond later tonight."

He ignored her, letting her prattle on while he covertly observed the scene at the gazebo. Obviously, Rachel and McMurtry were engaged in an intense discussion, and he had a gut feeling that the outcome of the powwow would be crucial for his own destiny.

"I've been trying to find the proper time to bring this up, Rachel." From the tone of his voice, Rachel knew he would accept no more polite put-offs or annoying interruptions. It was a time of reckoning between them.

"I believe I know what you're about to say, and I wish you wouldn't." Nervously, she paced the perimeter of the octagon-shaped gazebo, skimming her fingertips along the bannister.

He followed her, clasping her shoulders and drawing her back against him. "I can offer you an alternative, Rachel. No more struggling alone. No more worries. I've had a thing for you for years. You know that." His lips sought the sleek curve of her neck. Involuntarily, she stiffened at their foreign touch.

"Dammit!" he cried, then roughly pivoted her around, frustration glinting in his stormy eyes. "Why don't you want me? Yancy never made you happy. All he ever brought you was misery. I can give you things he never dreamed of. You don't have to be madly in love with me. Hell! You don't have to be in love with me at all! I've wanted you since we were kids and used to neck down by the pond."

His eyes were becoming glazed, and his breathing grew ragged. To herself, she began to question her own judgment about his gentlemanly character.

"I can provide whatever you might want or need, Rachel. All I ask in return is what I've always desired. I can guarantee that if you'll satisfy me, you'll be amply rewarded for my sole privileges to you." Before she could recover from the shock of his blunt proposition, he pinned her in his arms, grinding his pelvis against hers and bruising her lips with a savage kiss.

She ground the spiked heel of her shoe into his instep, at which he instantly released her. "Are you out of your mind?" she gasped. "I've never heard of such a disgusting tradeoff. If and when I choose to sleep with a man, it won't be because he bribed me to do so. Yancy may not have been the most reliable man, but he certainly had a hell of a lot more horse sense than you."

"Is that a fact?" he challenged, smirking at her naïveté. "Maybe you ought to know just what a louse Yancy actually was. It's no wonder he let the farm go to pot. Hell! He was studding half the women in the county."

"You're a liar," she spat. "You're just defaming Yancy's memory out of spite."

He narrowed the space between them, and it was then that she perceived the cold confidence in his face. "Am I?" he mocked. "Ask most anybody. Better yet, confront Marybeth Waylon or Desiree Sayer with what I've just told you and watch 'em squirm. Have you forgotten how Marybeth carried on at his funeral? You only lost a worthless husband; she lost a lover who promised her the moon. According to her, they were to have run off together in the spring."

Numbly Rachel endured Jonas's lashing. Although her mind was reeling with pain from his cruelty, in her heart she knew he spoke the truth. Long before Yancy's death she had had her suspicions about his indiscriminate carousing, but she had had no actual proof. Not a soul had breathed so much as a whisper about his extramarital activities to her, and Yancy had flatly denied any misconduct on his part. Why now, after his death, did Jonas choose to assassinate his character? "Is it giving you some sort of perverse satisfaction to say these ugly things to me? What kind of man are you?"

"I don't mean to hurt you, Rachel, but it's time you quit burying your head in the sand and faced reality. Yancy was no good, and you're in over your head with that farm. No way are you going to make it work. Don't be so damned stubborn. For God's sake, I'm offering you lifelong security. Be smart for once. Accept the arrangement I've suggested before everything comes tumbling down around you."

She wanted to scream. She wanted to cry. She wanted to throw herself at Jonas and scratch his smug face raw. But she did none of those things. She hadn't the strength. Instead, she rallied herself and bluffed him with a cool and reviling look. "You're sorrier than Yancy on his worst day. I've no intention of marrying you, now or ever. I think your ex-wife must've warped your mind about women. Believe it or not, some of us do have principles." Shaking with both outrage and apprehension, she fled the gazebo, shouting back over her shoulder, "I want no more credit from you, Jonas McMurtry. The interest you expect is too damned steep."

"So, honey, what do you say? Are you interested in a moonlight dip in the pond?" Desiree slipped her hand around the nape of his neck, then ran her tapered nails up into his hair.

He grabbed her wrist and held her at bay. "Whatever sick game you're playing, I've had my fill. Believe me, Desiree, you're out of your league when it comes to slick maneuvering. I've got the scars to prove it."

She wrenched free of his grip and rubbed her smarting wrist. "I want to go home right this minute," she fumed.

"It'd be my pleasure to take you," he agreed readily, following her voluptuous figure through the crowd to the pickup out back.

They exchanged not another word throughout the drive to her house. Only after she'd climbed from the pickup unassisted and slammed the door shut did she bid him adieu. "My fondest wish is that you skid off the road and end up as dead as Yancy. You're a bigger bastard than he ever was."

"That may be, but I'm a better driver." He geared into reverse and sped off, musing to himself during the ride home what a damned shame it was that she and McMurtry hadn't struck up a close acquaintanceship. They were definitely two of a kind.

As he passed through the gates of the farm, he was surprised to see the kitchen light still on. His first thought was that something might be amiss with Meggie. He quickly parked and took the steps two at a time in his haste. Much to his amazement, it was Rachel he encountered when he bolted through the back screen door.

"Is Meggie okay?" he blurted.

"She's fine and sleeping like a babe." Her easy manner had a tranquilizing effect on him. "I'm fixing myself a toddy. Would you like one?"

Relief flooded his face as he removed his jacket and slung it across the back rung of a chair. "I could use one," he replied, taking a seat and watching her go through the familiar motions.

"Me, too," she murmured, keeping her eyes averted.

"You're home early." He left the observation dangling.

"Bubba Atkins gave me a lift." She set the toddies onto the table and collapsed into a chair.

"Oh," he said, idly swirling the whipped cream with a spoon.

She sipped the toddy, offering no explanation.

The clock on the walk ticked off another minute before she spoke again. "Jonas asked me to marry him tonight."

His heart stilled in his chest.

"I refused him."

A faint beat reaffirmed that he'd survived the shock. "Why didn't you take him up on his offer?" Feeling steady enough to raise the cup, he took a reviving gulp.

She eased back into her chair, removing the combs from her hair and shaking free the silky strands. "I don't love him" was all she answered.

A spark of hope rekindled inside of him. "That's the best reason I know of not to accept."

She finished off the toddy, asking, "Want another?"

He'd never known her to drink so purposefully. It was as if she wanted to blot out an unspecified pain. "Sure, why not?" He passed her his cup and noted the excessive amount of bourbon she added to her own. Something more than Jonas's proposal was bothering her. He patiently waited, feeling that in her own good time she would divulge the reason for her despair.

She shivered at the burn of the bourbon, but she drank it all the same. "Do you think it's unrealistic of me to think I can make this farm turn a cash flow again?"

The question took him off guard. He studied her, noting the signs of stress in her face. "I think you've made a fine start at doing precisely that. In a few more weeks you'll harvest a bumper cotton crop. You should be able to catch up on your delinquent accounts and still have some left over to buy seed for winter wheat."

She raised her eyes to his, and he could read the self-doubt and anxiety within them. "Jonas doesn't believe I can do it. He pressured me to accept an arrangement between us." At Ben's befuddled expression, she took a

147

swig and elaborated. "Do you remember when you suggested that I could make a tradeoff for the shingles?"

He nodded, embarrassed. "I was angry, Rachel. I never believed you would compromise yourself."

"Well, I can assure you that Jonas thinks otherwise. In return for my satisfying him, he'd guarantee me lifelong security. No more worries. No more busting my butt from sunup to sundown. I'd be a lady of leisure." She slammed the empty cup onto the table furiously.

Good old Jonas hadn't disappointed him. Ben had known he was an ass, and now the idiot had proven him right. "What exactly did you say to him?"

"I told him he was out of his warped mind. That I don't sleep with a man for gratuities." The liquor was going to her head. She felt out of control, and it frightened her.

"There's something more, isn't there, Rachel?" He shoved aside their cups and, without thinking, brushed back the hair from her cheek.

She caught his hand, smoothing the calloused flesh between her palms. "You know me so well," she murmured. "It wasn't just Jonas's proposition that bothered me. It was the hateful things he said about Yancy. I suspected my husband had made a habit out of cheating on me, but until tonight no one ever confirmed it. Even when you know it's the truth, it still tears you up inside to hear the sleazy details."

At his silence, she looked up and smiled sadly. "You've known for some time, haven't you?"

"It's spiteful gossip, Rachel."

"No, it's very true. It's sweet of you to try and shield me, but it's not necessary." She released his hand and stood. The room spun, and she gripped the chair to steady herself.

Instantly Ben was beside her, swooping her up into his safe and strong arms.

She rested her dizzy head on his shoulder, blaming her weakness on the toddy. "Too much bourbon," she whispered as he carried her upstairs.

He kissed her forehead and gently cradled her closer. "Not so, honey. Just too much to contend with all at once."

"You're not planning to take advantage of me, are you, Ben?"

He tucked her into her bed with an amused "No, babe. It's not my style to take advantage of beautiful widows or helpless orphans. Rest. You'll feel much better in the morning."

CHAPTER TEN

Rachel was able to cope much better in the morning. The air was brisk and cleansing as she stood on the porch enjoying a steamy cup of coffee. She rationalized oversleeping for church with the thought that it must be the Lord's will that she give her wounded pride a chance to heal before mingling with her neighbors. How many of them had clucked their tongues and pitied her behind her back? She would like to believe they had held their peace out of respect for her feelings, but she knew there were those—like Jonas—whose motives were anything but charitable.

Ben had taken Meggie fishing to give Rachel a little privacy. Sometimes his thoughtfulness was truly amazing, as was the gentlemanly way he'd conducted himself last night; his behavior had been above reproach.

He'd become so much more than just an extra pair of hands around the place. He'd been her perfect lover, and he remained her trusted friend.

It suddenly became clear to her that it didn't matter if you actually said the words *I love you* aloud if you felt it in your heart. It didn't matter if you vowed "I can't let myself care for you" if you already did. It didn't matter if you lay with a man once or a thousand times, because if it's magical, as it was with Ben, you would never forget it and you could never deny the specialness. God help her, she had fallen in love with him. She sure as hell hadn't meant to, but it had happened all the same. And soon he would be leaving Mesquite Junction, never knowing that along with his few belongings he would also take her heart.

She perched herself on the porch railing and gazed off at the fields. They'd done a good job together. She couldn't remember a better crop. Jonas was dead wrong if he believed for one second that she would throw in the towel at this late stage. She'd sell or hock almost every personal possession she owned first. She was going to make it. Just a few more weeks and one good harvest were all that separated her from accomplishing her purpose. Thanks to Ben, she'd survive to plant again in the seasons to come. This farm would not become another statistic. It would not be reclaimed by overgrowth and the Farm Credit Administration. No, this good and independent way of life would not perish.

"Amen," she whispered, her spirit full of gratitude and hope. At the recognizable backfire of Bubba Atkins's old pickup coming up the road, she peered into the distance and was surprised by his unexpected turn onto her property.

Waving hello, she slipped into the kitchen for a refill and to pour him a cup. He was waiting for her in the yard when she returned.

"Missed ya at services this morning. Everything okay?" he inquired, taking the mug from her gratefully and seating himself on the steps.

"Everything's fine, Bubba. I just felt lazy this morning." She sat down beside him, smiling at his appreciative sigh when he tasted the coffee. "How goes it with you?"

"Same as always. The missus is startin' her fall preservin', and I'm gettin' ready to harvest."

She nodded and focused on the cotton field.

"Ya got a dandy crop this year, Rachel."

"That I do, Bubba," she said proudly.

"Mine's only fair to middlin', but it'll get me by, I expect. Looks like that hired hand I sent ya worked out pretty good." He cocked a brow and cast her a sideways glance.

"You're a slick old fox, Bubba Atkins. I suppose you felt obliged to mention my recent widowhood to him before you dropped him on my doorstep?" She shook her head at his sheepish grin.

"Now, don't go jumpin' to the wrong conclusion, Rachel. I wasn't implyin' that you'd be interested in anythin' more than a strong back. In fact, I warned him you was a mite peculiar and the chances were slim that ya'd hire him on." He chewed his tobacco, then took aim and spat the brown juice into the bushes.

"The only reason you think I'm peculiar is because I didn't behave like folks around here thought I should. I didn't waste time mourning my fickle husband, and I didn't sell out." Her chin set stubbornly.

"Ya gotta admit that it was a risky move, Rachel. Ya could've lost all you own," he pointed out between sips of coffee.

"I never felt that I had a choice," she answered simply. "This farm was mine, not Yancy's. It's been in my family for three generations. God willing, it'll be passed on to Meggie."

"God willin'," he agreed. "That's the main reason I came out here, Rachel. There's something I thought ya ought to know."

His somber tone made her uneasy. Bubba wasn't one

to take much seriously, so she assumed that whatever he'd come to say weighed heavy on his mind.

"You'd better just tell me what it is straight out. I can tell the news isn't good."

"Jake Simmons killed hisself last night. He tried to make it look like an accident, but nobody's much believing it."

She was stunned. The Simmons farm was definitely in worse straits than hers, but it was so close to harvest! It was unbelievable that Jake could not have held on a little longer. "But why would he do such a thing?"

Bubba spat again, then stared at the ground. "Probably because the sheriff posted his place for auction. It's supposed to take place next Saturday. 'Pears to me Jake decided that if his family collected his insurance money, they might be able to postpone the auction with a guarantee to pay their debts. Worst thing is, it looks like his suicide was in vain. According to talk, the auction's gonna go off as scheduled, and because of the suspicious circumstances the insurance company is balking at paying the claim."

"Dammit!" She vaulted to her feet, standing rigid and fending off the apprehension swelling within her chest. "It's not fair. Couldn't the jackals have waited a few lousy weeks?"

Bubba shrugged his stooped shoulders. He hadn't an answer for the injustice. "That's what folks were askin' themselves at church today. I suppose the most we can hope is that his troubled soul is at peace now." He finished off the coffee and stood. "I just thought you'd wanna know. There ain't nothin' we can do, except maybe be there Saturday to give Sarah and the kids some moral support."

He patted her on the shoulder. "Wish I had the money

to buy that idle acreage from you, Rachel. It's a damned shame to let good farmland be overrun with mesquite trees. I know ya'd rest easier with the extra cash in the bank, but times being as hard as they are, I can't risk strappin' my own savings."

She appreciated both his dilemma and his sweet intention. "I'll be all right, Bubba. My creditors aren't pulling the rug out from under me yet. In a few more weeks I'll be ginning my cotton, and like you said, it's a dandy crop. You forget, I'm not only peculiar, I'm tough. Thanks for dropping by and letting me know about Jake. I'll pay my respects to Sarah and the kids, and they can count on my being at their side during the auction next Saturday."

"There's a damned war going on, Rachel. If things don't lighten up, there may not be many independents like us left. There'll be more casualties in the days ahead. Mark my words." He shook his shaggy head and ambled toward the battered pickup.

"Maybe not," she called after him. "It's been a good growing season. Maybe things are finally taking a turn for the better." She didn't know who she was trying to convince—herself or Bubba.

"The season ain't over yet, Rachel," he reminded her, climbing into the pickup and gunning it. "If I don't see Ben before he moseys off, tell him I said for him to take care of hisself and that I'm bettin' it'll rain again before harvest time. I can smell it in the air."

"Sure, I'll give him the message." She had to shout to make herself heard over the blast of the pickup.

"I don't know why you want to put yourself through this," Ben muttered beneath his breath as they weaved through the farmers who had assembled for the auction.

Most were neighbors, but several faces in the crowd were those of strangers—vultures who had come to pick the carcass of the dead farm.

Impatience shortened her stride and temper. "These are more than just my neighbors, and they're part of a bigger tragedy than just the loss of a good man and one small farm. It isn't just equipment and property that's being sold off today; it's a way of life. Anytime one of us gets cut, all of us bleed. I can't stop the misery that's going to take place here this afternoon, but I can damned sure grieve with Sarah and the kids. I want them to know that somebody cares, and I want them to be proud of what Jake stood for."

"I was only thinking of how hard this would be on you." Ever since she had heard the news of the imminent auction, Rachel had been withdrawn and edgy. Late at night he could hear her pacing in her room, and he often found her keeping a vigil at the fields before dawn. She was worried sick that some unforeseen disaster would strike her, too. After Jake Simmons's suicide, the rumor that her farm was next in line for foreclosure gathered momentum. She wasn't deaf or dumb; the talk had reached her ears, and she knew it wasn't totally unfounded. Although harvest time was approaching, so was the postponed deadline on her past-due mortgage.

"I appreciate the concern, but I'm quite all right," she insisted.

They both knew she was lying, that she was wound so tight that at any given moment she could easily explode.

Further argument was useless. Ben decided it best to remain low-key and available in case she wasn't as strong as she thought.

The auction began right on time. At high noon the first piece of machinery—a caterpillar—was put up for bid. A misty-eyed Sarah Simmons stood in the doorway of her soon-to-be-vacated home and observed the proceedings from afar, but her fifteen-year-old son paced by the fence, venting his rage by ramming a fist into his palm over and over again.

The disgruntled farmers bowed their heads as the auctioneer coaxed, "Come on, folks. I don't like this any better than you, but it's gotta be done. Will somebody start the bidding at two hundred dollars?"

Rachel saw Sarah reel and clutch the doorjamb for support. The teen-age boy folded his arms over a fence post and buried his head to hide his tears. Something inside her snapped at the sight.

"*Why* must it be done?" she shouted from the middle of the crowd. "You may have the right to take away the Simmons's property and possessions, but we don't have to help you do it!"

The pent-up frustration that everyone present shared was expressed in a concurring grumble.

Ben immediately realized the potential danger of a riot. Although these people were generally mild-mannered and God-fearing, they were also fatigued and dispirited from struggling like salmon against an upstream current. Rachel wasn't the only one who wanted to lash out at the injustice of grain embargos and escalating interest rates. And soon she wasn't the only voice crying out.

The sheriff took charge, aiming his remarks at Rachel in particular. "Now, let's keep this civil, folks. I don't want any trouble here today. The man's only doing his job, and you're out of line, Rachel."

Ben tried to grab her, but she slapped his hand away and pushed her way to the front. "Well, so maybe I am," she challenged. "But I'll tell you something, sheriff. If I'm out of line, this whole country's out of whack!" She

156

turned and faced her neighbors. "You, Swen Bishop"—
she pointed a finger at a ruddy-faced Swede—"would you
be the first to bid on the caterpillar of a man who brought
you groceries when your account was too high at Peter-
son's and your pantry was bare? Or you, Bubba Atkins"
—her accusing finger swept to the old man—"would you
do it after Jake plowed your fields when you fell from a
rafter in the barn and crushed a vertebra in your back?"

"Stop firing things up, Rachel," the sheriff warned.

She spun on him, her almond eyes ablaze with defiance. "Maybe things need to be fired up. Maybe it's time
to quit acting like lambs going to the slaughter."

Cheers went up behind her, the crowd rallying and
closing in.

Ben feared that if he didn't act quickly, a major upris-
ing could ignite. He shoved his way to behind Rachel,
unsure of exactly what he intended to do but convinced
that some drastic measure must be used to avoid a lynch-
ing of the cowering auctioneer and the unpopular sheriff.

"You're leaving me no choice, Rachel. I'm gonna run
you in for disorderly conduct if you don't back off. And I
do mean now," the sheriff threatened.

The ultimatum only seemed to spur Rachel on. No one
but Ben knew that she was teetering on the brink of hysteria. She struck a bullish pose, daring him to make good
his threat. "Fine, you just try and—"

Ben's hand clamped over her mouth, muffling the dis-
respectful retort she would've uttered. In a lightning-
quick move, he picked her up and carried her away.
"There's no need to do anything hasty, sheriff. Rachel's
just a bit high-strung today, is all."

She balked like a mule, but he marched through the
crowd. Not a soul interfered. Her curses grew fainter as
he carried her to the pickup and deposited her inside.

157

"You had no right to manhandle me like that." She tried to wriggle from the cab of the truck.

"I have every right." He shoved her against the seat and pinned her with a firm hand. "I don't intend to have to explain to Meggie why her mother is stewing in the county jail. I sympathize with your cause, Rachel, but it's not worth a two-hundred-dollar fine and sixty days on a pea farm, not to mention the fact that we've got a damned harvest to make. What good will it do the Simmonses for you to sacrifice yourself?"

She leaned her head back, closed her eyes, and ceased to struggle. "You're right," she conceded with a deep sigh. "I warned you that I could be unreasonable at times."

Sensing that she was regaining herself, he released her, shut the passenger door of the truck, hustled to the driver's side, and climbed in.

"I'm sorry if I embarrassed you," she apologized as he started up the truck. "Something inside me just couldn't let it be."

"You're a lady of strong principles, Rachel. One day there will be a better time and place to express them."

He tried to coax a smile from her, but she turned her head to keep him from seeing the tears welling in her eyes. She felt foolish and inexplicably wary, as if some phantom menace were stalking her. She couldn't confide in Ben. It wouldn't be right. He'd assumed far too much responsibility for her problems as it was. Yet she couldn't dismiss the nagging worry that it would take only one unexpected setback to wipe her out. Was she merely identifying too closely with the Simmonses misfortune? she wondered silently. Or was her anxiousness the understandable result of the constant strain? Dear Lord, don't let it be a premonition, she prayed.

She'd been at it for hours—sitting at the kitchen table, riffling through the unpaid invoices, and refiguring her finances. No matter how she juggled the figures, the result was the same: without the working capital from the coming harvest to bail her out of debt, the farm was doomed. She'd exhausted all her resources. Although she'd known all along that everything hinged on the harvest, she'd hoped to discover some loophole that she might utilize if all else failed. No such miracle was contained within the deeds, accounts, and farm aid literature she had studied.

Ben came down the steps from tucking Meggie in to find her elbow deep in past-due notices, her forehead propped in her palms and her fingers tangled in her hair.

Wordlessly he picked up her sweater, wrapped it around her shoulders, and raised her from the chair. "Let's take a walk. The fresh air will clear your head."

"I need to try to sort this out."

"Later," he said, giving her a gentle nudge toward the screen door.

They walked in silence for a while. Only the distant baying of a coonhound at the moon broke the peace of the autumn night.

Finally, Ben spoke. "Take my advice, Rachel. I've been where you are, and I can tell you from experience that the only thing you'll accomplish by trying to second-guess any and every possibility is to give yourself ulcers. You've done your best. In a few days we'll gin the cotton. In the meantime there's nothing you can do but wait."

"I can pray." She hugged her cardigan sweater tighter about herself.

"That's always an option, I suppose." He shoved his

hands deep into the pockets of his jeans and gazed up at the hazy moon.

"I can appreciate how hard it must have been for you just before your business failed."

"I wouldn't ever want to relive that time in my life. Jeanette served me with divorce papers on the same day I declared chapter eleven. I don't think I drew a sober breath for a month."

"Funny. It's hard for me to picture you not in control." She glanced at his profile, trying to imagine him tipsy.

"Why?"

She shrugged, murmuring, "Maybe because you seem so even-keeled all the time."

"I did a hundred-and-eighty-degree turn after Dallas. When you lose everything at once, there's not a whole hell of a lot that rocks you anymore."

"Frankly, the thought of having this land repossessed scares me to death. All I know is farming. I doubt I'd be very good at much else, and unlike you, I'm not sure I've got the kind of grit it takes to begin all over again."

He paused, gently taking her by her shoulders and turning her to face him. "You have something I didn't. Something I would've gladly traded the fortune I lost for. Love. No matter what happens, you'll always have Meggie. She can't be taken from you. Oil empires crumble and family farms disappear, but love can't be repossessed, and it's the only true asset in this whole damned world."

She yearned to tell him that he, too, was loved. But the words stuck in her throat—her damnable pride was in the way. How could she phrase it without humbling herself? "Someone should've been there to love you when you needed it so much." Involuntarily, she reached out and caressed his cheek.

160

The night's shadows hid his betraying wince. Although he so much wanted to interpret the tender gesture as something more than empathy, he was afraid to believe it. He felt her hand tremble, and he mistakenly interpreted it as a shiver. "There's a nip in the air tonight. Why don't we head back, and I'll try my hand at fixing us a toddy?"

Like a moth who'd been attracted to a hypnotic flame and then singed by the fire, she retracted her hand. "Sure. That'd be nice for a change."

They lapsed into a strained silence once more, and on returning to the house he prepared the toddies with only minimal instructions from her.

"It doesn't taste exactly the same." Ill at ease and fighting an impulse to lean over and lick the frothy whipped cream from her delectable lips, he resorted to small talk.

"It's very good." She forced a smile, putting up a brave front for his sake.

"I'd grown kind of accustomed to sharing these toddies with you. I'll miss them." He stared into his cup for fear that she would detect his greatest weakness—her.

"So will I, Ben." The words seemed so inept. They were spoken fondly when, in fact, she loved him madly.

He couldn't sit with her any longer, not without making a damned fool out of himself. "Well, I guess I'll hit the sack," he muttered inanely.

She nodded, unable to trust herself to speak.

" 'Night, Rachel." He chanced a glance at her, but her downcast eyes were riveted to the paperwork.

She swallowed hard. " 'Night," she uttered softly. No sooner had he walked from the room than tears began to trickle down her cheeks. She didn't even realize she was crying until a sob welled in her throat. *Don't do it! Don't fall apart now,* she told herself. She laid her head on the clutter of paperwork on the table and shuddered as the dammed-up emotion within her burst.

The walls were thin. The sound of her crying penetrated to Ben's cubbyhole. The only thing that kept him from leaving the smothering confines of his room was the knowledge that she needed to release the tension and that his presence would only make her repress it. It didn't cross his mind that he was in any way responsible for her tears. Still, restraining himself from encroaching on her privacy was the hardest thing he'd ever done. He paced. He cursed. He sat on the edge of the bed, raked his hands through his hair, and gritted his teeth. As a last resort, he prayed.

"If you exist like she believes, help her get through this. She's a good woman who's had more than her share of troubles lately. I've done all I can. It's up to you now."

Her crying ceased, and soon he heard her climb the stairs. Stretching his lean torso out on the bed, he stared up into the darkness, wondering if it was coincidence or perhaps, just possibly, there might be something to this ambiguous thing she called faith.

CHAPTER ELEVEN

Ben was jolted awake by a thunderous racket that sounded like a herd of buffalo stampeding across the roof. Springing from the bed, he jerked on his jeans and bolted from the room, colliding with Rachel in the hall.

Her face was ashen and her eyes frantic as she identified the source of the sound. "A hailstorm," she groaned. "Why me? Jesus! Why me?"

Before he could offer an opinion, she staggered dazedly into the kitchen, cracked the screen door, and looked on helplessly as the golf ball–size hail bounced off the roof and pummeled her crop. The freak storm lasted approximately five minutes, but in that short time it leveled the cotton crop and destroyed whatever chance she'd had to save her farm.

She stood paralyzed. When the storm ebbed, so did her spirit. Ben wished with all his heart that he could think of something, anything, consoling to say. But as he glanced beyond the window at the devastated fields, the only words that came to mind were either inadequate or too crude to utter.

Meggie came sleepwalking into the kitchen, dragging her teddy bear by an arm and tripping on the hem of her flannel gown. "What is it, Mama?" she asked, yawning.

Rachel did not answer the child. Catatonically, she

walked out the door and toward the fields, her robe billowing in the gusty wind.

Ben picked Meggie up in his arms and stepped out onto the porch, explaining, "A hailstorm hit, Meggie."

"Is that what those giant round ice cubes are called?"

"Yes." His concerned eyes followed Rachel as she made her way to the edge of the ravaged fields.

"They sure made a mess." The tot's assessment was an understatement. What had once been bountiful rows of cotton looked more like a battlefield now.

Bubba Atkins's backfiring pickup swerved onto the Daniels property and screeched to a halt in the drive. Ben descended the steps with Meggie still clutched in his arms. The two men exchanged knowing glances, and Atkins murmured, "How's about ya coming and havin' breakfast with old Bubba and the missus this mornin', Meggie?"

"I dunno." She looked to Ben, sensing the old man's urgency and unsure if she should accept.

"Go with Bubba, honey." He relinquished her into Atkins's care. "Your mother and I need some time to set things straight around here."

"You won't be too long coming to fetch me, will ya, Ben?" Her eyes were filled with apprehension as Bubba deposited her into the pickup.

"I'll be by as soon as I can," he assured her as Bubba took his arm and pulled him aside for a private word.

"Freakiest thing I ever saw. The damned thing hopscotched across thirty miles of farmland. Missed me, but it hit some others as hard as Rachel. How's she takin' it?"

"Not well. I'd appreciate it if you could keep Meggie for the day. I'll drop her off a change of clothes the first chance I get." Ben nodded toward the field where Rachel sat huddled on the ground.

"Be glad to." Bubba shook his head and gave Ben a bolstering slap on the back. "It's a damned shame this had to happen to her. Wish there was something more I could do."

"Yeah. It seems the God she so trusts turns his back on those that need it most."

Although Bubba was taken aback by his sacrilege, he offered no argument. "I better get the young'n over to my place. Tell Rachel not to worry about imposin'. My old hen will be thrilled at having a chick to cluck over once again."

Meggie leaned out the window and blew Ben a parting kiss as the oil-guzzling truck backed out onto the black-topped road.

It was a damp, chilly morning, yet even though he was barefoot and shirtless, Ben was oblivious to all else but Rachel's pain. As he approached her huddled figure, he wondered what on earth he could do or say to ease her sorrow. He squatted beside her, surveying the damage and sighing at the disheartening sight.

She finally spoke as she picked up a mauled cotton boll that was filthy with silt and cupped it in her hand. "Why don't I feel anything?" she muttered.

"You're in shock," he replied, rubbing her shoulders.

"After all our work and my many prayers, this is all we have to show." She raised her hand, then let the mutilated boll fall onto the soggy ground. "I should feel something. Anger, grief, disgust . . ."

"Try cold." He stood, clasped her hands, and hauled her onto her feet. "You're sitting in a pool of ice water and asking for a bout with pneumonia."

She wasn't aware that her lips were purple or that the

165

hail marsh had soaked her robe to her knees. Disbelievingly, her blank eyes skimmed the emptiness where an abundant crop had once stood. "It was quick and painless, wasn't it?" she said chokingly.

He realized she was traumatized and shivering. He cloaked her within his arms, holding her numb body fast against his warm flesh and smoothing her wind-tousled hair.

"I won't be able to pay you. I'm so sorry . . . so sorry," she repeated over and over again as he swung her into his arms and carried her away from the devastation.

Only when she was cradled in his arms like a baby did she begin to cry. His grip on her tightened with each sob that wracked her body. He managed to open the screen door and take the hall steps without slackening his hold on her.

Once inside the bathroom, he sat with her curled in his lap on the edge of the tub and turned on the hot water one-handed.

"We've got to get you warm, babe," he explained, slipping the robe from her shoulders, supporting her as they stood, and letting it slink to the floor. She closed her eyes as he drew the silk nightshirt over her head and inched her lace panties down her legs.

At his retreat to test the water, she panicked. Her eyes fluttered open and were filled with entreaty as she stammered, "D-D-Don't leave me alone, Ben," through chattering teeth.

He clutched her hand reassuringly and guided her into the tub. "Lay here and soak while I fix us some hot coffee."

Vaguely she sensed that she should be embarrassed at his tending to her, stripped of her clothes and pride, but she needed him too much at this moment to care. He'd thoughtfully added bubble bath to the hot water, and she inched down beneath the camouflaging bubbles with a timid nod.

It seemed as if she'd only closed her eyes for a minute or two when he was back in the bathroom, carrying a fluffy towel and dry robe. Yet instead of leaving her to her hygiene in the steamy room, he knelt at the side of the tub and began lathering a sponge.

"You don't have to do this." The feeble protest sounded even weaker than she felt.

"I want to" was all he replied, cupping her neck with a hand, gently raising her up, swabbing her back in lazy arcs, then rinsing away her woes with repeated squeezes of hot water from the sponge.

He lathered and massaged her limbs, then gently buffed her face until life began to trickle back into her body. "You're so good to me, Ben," she murmured, letting her head rest against the back of the tub as he rubbed the sponge along her tense neck and shoulders.

He spoke not a word but discarded the sponge, taking the bar of soap in his large hand and slipping it under the water and over her breasts. She sucked in a deep breath and opened her eyes to his. Slowly and easily, the soap slicked back and forth over her blossoming nipples, but she did not shy away from the intimacy or the hunger gleaming in his hazel eyes. Instead, she reached up an arm, dripping bubbles down his bare back, cupped his neck with her palm, and drew his eager mouth to her wet lips.

The water lapped rhythmically as his hand and the bar of soap washed over her stomach, hips, and buttocks. The motion in itself was trancelike, and his kiss transported her beyond the inhibiting boundaries of modesty.

He was so loving, so giving, so healing. And she was so empty, so needing, so sick at heart.

The creamy bar of soap slipped between her thighs. She gasped, her fingers tangling in his hair. "I'm getting warmer," she moaned, grazing her lips deliriously along his cheek and down his neck as a wanton warmth spread through her.

The feather kisses she strung across his broad shoulders became urgent. "There's not room for us both in this tub. My bed would be much more accommodating," she suggested.

She felt the instantaneous tensing of his muscles and was confused. His divine motion beneath the water ceased. He cupped her face between his palms and stared deep into her eyes.

"I'm not trying to take advantage, Rachel. You're all mixed up right now, and you don't know what you feel. I want you, but—"

She placed a finger on his lips. "I'll dry off and you can bring the coffee up here. I don't want to go downstairs just yet. Please, Ben, let me borrow your strength this last time. Let's close the door and shut out the world for a few hours."

He'd gladly be her citadel for a lifetime if she so desired. Brushing her lips with a gossamer kiss, he deferred to her need with a comprehending nod, then gave her a few minutes of privacy.

By the time he returned upstairs with the coffee, she sat propped in the four-poster bed, swaddled in an heirloom quilt and smelling of sweet talc. She looked so adorable—her skin was still flushed from the hot bath, her hair was piled atop her head, bound by a pink satin ribbon, and wet ringlets spilled around her fresh-scrubbed face.

As he handed her the mug, she turned back the corner of the quilt in silent invitation. Wordlessly, he stripped, and joined her in the antique bed. She moved closer, resting the back of her head in the crook of his shoulder and sipping the coffee.

"Feeling better?" he murmured, nestling a cheek against her fragrant curls and idly stroking her arm.

She raised up, setting aside the mug on the nightstand and turning to him with misty-eyed need. "Hold me tight, Ben, so tight that I can't feel anything but you."

Instantly, his sheltering arms enfolded her, and they sank deeper into the feather mattress. He lent her his love like a downy bunting to insulate her against a cold, harsh world.

"Tell me it's going to be all right. Make me believe it, even though I know it's not true," she begged.

Her plea tugged at his heart. Tenderly he claimed her trembling lips and sheathed her body with his own.

"Shh, don't cry, babe," he crooned, tasting the salt from her tears as he kissed her cheeks, her chin, her forehead.

Although his face was a blur, the heat from his lithe body and his musky male scent were reassuring. She linked her arms around his neck, smiling weakly up at him. "I am blessed in one way. In the midst of my trials, God saw fit to provide you."

"I hardly think I'm a blessing." He caressed her thigh and swathed the hollow of her throat in lingering kisses.

"Oh, but you are, Ben Eaton." A contented sigh escaped her.

The sigh was only a prelude to the incomparable satisfaction the vulnerable farm woman would reap from an unforgettable afternoon of lovemaking with her hired hand. Lovingly, he soothed her heartache, promising that things would work out. Unselfishly, he assumed her sorrow. Adoringly, he made love to her. And although she thought his pledge to save her farm from ruin was conceived of only the sweetest and most noble intentions, she did not believe that even Bennett Earl Eaton could work such a miracle.

She had fallen asleep in his arms after their love tryst. Ever so carefully, he eased from her side, tucked the quilt about her, dressed, and tiptoed from the room. By evening, he'd plowed under twenty acres of mutilated and worthless cotton plants and had retrieved Meggie from the Atkins place.

"What's Mama gonna do now?" Margaret Jane caught hold of his hand as they walked the fenceline separating what had once been productive acreage from mesquite-laden wasteland.

He stopped and surveyed the shrub forest. "I'll think of something," he said distractedly.

"Whatcha staring at? Ain't nothing out there but nasty old mesquite." She jiggled about and crossed her legs. "I gotta tee-tee, Ben," she complained.

He tweaked her ponytail and grinned. "Head on to the house, then. I'll be along in a minute."

Mother Nature's call was stronger than her desire to know what he was speculating so hard about. She left him to wander the fenceline alone.

When he finally returned to the house, he was stunned to find a veritable feast awaiting him. During his absence Rachel had prepared an honest-to-God homecooked supper—honey-glazed ham, yams, garden green beans, sourdough rolls, and the richest, most delicious pecan pie ever to cross his palate.

"It's the least I could do," she said with a shy smile,

truly delighted and yet embarrassed by his barrage of compliments.

"You never cease to amaze me, Rachel," he whispered as he helped her clear the table. "If I were to stay on for a score more seasons, I doubt I'd ever know what next to expect from you."

Her heart rejoiced at the slim possibility that he might actually be contemplating an extended stay. "I don't think that's necessarily bad," she murmured low, so Meggie couldn't hear. "People tend to become indifferent when they take each other for granted."

Meggie slammed shut her grammar book and leaned back into a chair with a huffy snort. "I can't do it!" she proclaimed dramatically, obstinately folding her arms across her chest. "I might as well quit school. I'm a failure."

Rachel smothered a smile and came to see what major adversity had beset her daughter. "We Danielses are not quitters, Margaret Jane. Now, open your book, and we'll tackle this together." She pulled up a chair and began to study the material.

Ben stepped out onto the porch to smoke an after-dinner cheroot and engage in a bit of pondering of his own. He struck a match and inhaled thoughtfully on the slim cigar, then extinguished the flame and gazed intently in the direction of the mesquite jungle. Perhaps, just perhaps, he might have a solution to Rachel's dilemma. It was damned sure worth a try. He had sworn never again to become involved in power plays and ticklish negotiations, but just this once he had to make an exception. He had to insure her and Meggie's stability before his departure; to do less would be as unconscionable as McMurtry's trying to coerce Rachel's love by making her dependent. But he had to act fast since Rachel's need for his labor would soon be over and he'd have no legitimate excuse to tarry longer.

At the screen door's creak, he snapped out of his musings and flipped the cheroot out into the yard. "Is our temperamental scholar feeling more confident?"

"I believe so." Rachel leaned against the railing at his booted feet.

"I have to go to Dallas tomorrow," he informed her, at which she cast him a wary glance.

"Business or pleasure?" was all she asked, although a stabbing fear that he might not return made her skin clammy. Why should he come back to this deplorable situation? she reasoned. Why should he care what became of a dowdy widow who had given him nothing but grief? Although he had been extraordinarily sensitive to her plight, she had no right to claim any more of his time, strength, or loyalty. This afternoon, out of compassion, he'd nursed her through the worst crisis of her life, but that certainly didn't mean that he intended to make a habit out of loving her.

"Business," he explained, afraid to raise her hopes prematurely by sharing his tentative solution.

"How long will you be gone?" She stood, bracing herself against the railing post and drawing her sweater closer about herself.

"I'm not sure. A few days, maybe. Can you do without the pickup that long?" He sensed her resigned withdrawal and wondered what had prompted it.

"I doubt I'll be going anywhere for a while, at least not until they come to evict me." She turned to go into the house, then paused and lavished a soft smile on him. "You're a special man, Ben Eaton. No matter what's in

172

store for me, when I recall the bitter of this season, I shall also remember the sweet of you."

Before he could react or respond to the unexpected sentiment, she vanished inside the house and took refuge in her room.

CHAPTER TWELVE

Hayden McCalister was a longtime friend and owner of one of the biggest steakhouse chains in the Southwest. If anyone would be interested in timber rights to two hundred acres of mesquite, it would be him. Yet Ben was hesitant to approach his old college chum with the deal. He would have to explain his interest in the declining farm, and worse yet, McCalister would be appalled that his ex-dorm mate who had once been the oil czar of Dallas was now picking cotton for minimal wages.

"You can go right in, Mr. Eaton." McCalister's prim and proper secretary surveyed him with a look of disdain.

He drew a deep breath, then marched through the private door. The plush office was reminiscent of his own palatial tower that had once loomed above the oil mecca.

"Well, I'll be goddamned!" Hayden eased back into his leather chair, staring at Ben as if he were Lazarus raised from the dead. "Where have you been for the past few years?" He took in Ben's appearance at a glance, then offered an opinion. "Slumming, I presume."

"It's good to see you too, Hayden." Ben extended a hand over the desk, then seated himself in the cushy chair that McCalister had offered with a curt nod of his head.

"Not a word from you in all this time, and then you

just casually waltz into my office and expect a brotherly welcome. Jesus! Earl, you could have told me you were in big trouble way back when. You knew I would have lent you whatever you needed to get your head above water again." Hayden's belated offer was sincere. He had been on safari in Kenya when the bottom fell out of Ben's empire, and by the time he returned, Ben had split from Dallas, leaving no forwarding address.

"I know, but it would've been a poor investment, Hayden. To tell you the truth, I think I was ready to cave in. In retrospect, I'm beginning to wonder if I ever had enough shark in me to survive in this sea of cutthroat crude. You wouldn't have done me a favor by bailing me out then." He lit up a cheroot. "But you could possibly be of assistance to me now."

"You want me to back you on some other endeavor?" Hayden asked, scowling and fanning the repugnant smoke. "You know how much I hate those stink bombs. It's the only thing Jeanette and I agreed about. By the way, I guess you heard she married again. It was quite a coup—a matrimonial merger with your arch-competitor, Buford Ettinger of Mesa Oil."

"True to character. Knowing Jeanette's opportunistic nature, I'm sure it occurred to her that she wouldn't even have to change the monogramming on the towels." Ben smirked, stubbing out the cheroot so as not to antagonize McCalister. He wanted him in the best humor possible when he presented the unorthodox proposal. "Listen, Hayden, I didn't come here to rehash the past. Actually, I have a business proposition for you."

McCalister assumed a more interested posture. "And here I thought you just missed me." He reached for the intercom, telling his secretary to clear his remaining appointments and requesting that lunch be sent in while they discussed the matter. "Okay, I got all afternoon. Let's talk."

Three hours and a bottle of bourbon later, Ben had what he had come for—a contract, hastily drawn up by McCalister's legal staff, guaranteeing Rachel Daniels a sizable sum in return for exclusive timber rights to her property. One of the primary ingredients of McCalister's successful steakhouse franchise was his "grilled over mesquite" claim. The bargain he and Ben had struck eliminated the costly middleman, thus saving McCalister a bundle and at the same time preserving the Daniels farm. Ben was quite pleased with the negotiations and more than a little drunk.

Hayden McCalister sat with his shirt-sleeves rolled up and his feet propped up on the desk. He, too, was looped. "So tell me the truth. Are you in love with this woman?"

Ben leaned forward in his chair to deposit his empty glass onto the desk, barely making the connection. "I adore her," he answered without the slightest reservation, the alcohol making him unusually candid.

"So what's next? Are you planning to settle down on the farm? Raise corn and snot-nosed kids?" Even in his inebriated condition, Hayden couldn't imagine Bennett Earl Eaton as a sodbuster.

"They grow cotton in the plains, Hayden," Ben corrected, hauling his cramped frame from the chair. "And as a matter of fact, that's exactly what I'd like to do, except that the lady in question isn't in the market for a husband."

"You mean to tell me that you're just going to hit the road again and never let the woman know you're crazy in love with her?" McCalister shook his head. "I don't understand you, Earl. Then what in the hell was this after-

176

noon all about? I thought you wanted to impress the woman by saving her farm."

"The days of my trying to impress a woman are long since over. You can't buy or manipulate love. If it doesn't develop in the natural course of events, then it's not meant to be."

"So you plan to just thumb off into the sunset, huh?"

Ben grinned at his sarcasm. Hayden always had a way with words. "Unless a miracle occurs between now and the end of the month, I suppose so. Thanks for all the help, Hayden. I'll get this contract back to you in a few days."

"Yeah, drop by again in a couple of years. Maybe next time we could collaborate on a travelogue for vagabonds?"

Ben laughed aloud, then bade him farewell.

It was late afternoon the following day when Ben returned to the farm.

"He's back," Meggie whooped, bolting through the screen door and running like a gazelle to the pickup. Although Rachel was every bit as eager as Meggie to see Ben, she took the time to check her appearance in the hall bath mirror and primp her hair. She didn't want to appear overly anxious, for then he might sense that she suspected he had taken a one-way hike, rather than a round trip, to Dallas. With the greatest of restraint, she resumed peeling vegetables for the stew she was preparing in the event of his return.

Meggie burst into the kitchen, proudly displaying a Dallas Cowboy jersey draped over her playclothes. "Look at what Ben brought me!" she exclaimed. "It's got Tony Dorsett's number." She stuck out her chest and pranced around like a peacock parading its tail. "Can I go show Cory, Mama? I'll ride my bike and be back in a flash."

"I guess it'd be all right, if you promise to watch out for traffic."

Before she could blink, Meggie was burning rubber up the road.

"That kid's got potential. Maybe you ought to enter her in the Indy 500 next year." Ben's spirits were as high as Meggie's as he walked to the stove and lifted the lid on the simmering stew meat. "Smells great. I don't know what prompted this cooking binge of yours, but I wish it had struck you a few months ago."

"Other than plowing under the fields, I haven't a whole heck of a lot to occupy me right now." She inched him aside, adding the vegetables to the pot and stirring the stew. "You're back sooner than I thought."

At the rate she was stirring, the stew would soon be mush. Ben took the wooden spoon from her hand and set it aside. "Come sit down. There's an important matter we need to discuss."

She reflected on his sober features for a second, then wiped her hands across the bib of her pinafore apron and perched stiffly on the edge of a chair. "You're leaving soon, aren't you, Ben?" Since his imminent departure was the only thing on her mind, she mistakenly believed he was on the verge of serving her formal notice.

He pulled the contract from his shirt pocket and laid it on the table. "Not until things are squared away here, Rachel." He searched for an encouraging sign from her —some small gesture that might give him cause to alter his departure schedule—but she merely stared at her lap, unaware of the vital document he had placed before her. "I think I may have found a solution to your problems in Dallas. This is a contract that, simply put, gives sole tim-

178

ber rights to that idle acreage of yours to McCalister Steakhouses, Inc., in exchange for a substantial sum. If you agree to the terms, the McCalister offer should more than cover your debts."

"Are you serious?" she gasped, scooping the contract from off the table and examining it closely. "Why on earth would anybody be interested in those mesquite-infested acres?"

"It's the mesquite that makes the land so valuable to McCalister. His restaurants are renowned for their open-pit grilled steaks. That wood you consider to be a nuisance is essential to McCalister's operation."

"I don't believe it! This is a godsend." She clutched the contract to her bosom. The dimpled smile he had been missing recently rematerialized. "I don't mean to sound ungrateful, but I'm wondering why, of all the sources at his disposal, would this Mr. McCalister choose my farm? I mean, the man doesn't even know me."

"He knows me" was Ben's modest reply. "We were dorm mates in college."

Her enthusiasm suddenly ebbed. "So that's why you made a rush trip to Dallas. It was a mission of mercy, so to speak. You traded on an old friendship to save the farm."

Ben recognized that familiar and stubborn inflection— her pride was offended. "Don't jump to conclusions, Rachel. Yes, McCalister and I are friends. And yes, that friendship may have gotten me in the door to see him. But the deal we struck was based on sound business sense, nothing more. McCalister needs your mesquite, and he's getting it for a fair price. That's the beginning and the end of it. So let's not quibble over ethics."

"You're positive?" she persisted, frowning dubiously.

179

She had the distinct feeling that under extenuating circumstances he could be as big a con artist as Meggie.

"I swear it." He hoped that just this once he could sneak something by her and she would accept a minor arbitration as good fortune.

Their eyes met, hers seeking to know if he was sincere, his willing her to act on the saving offer. "Where do I sign?" she asked at last.

He produced a pen from his pocket and showed her the specific pages that required her signature. Not until she had inscribed her name to the final page did he breathe easily. "Great. I'll send this by registered mail from Lubbock tomorrow, and you should be receiving a check within a week or two." He replaced the crucial contract in his pocket with a relieved grin.

"Who would've thought that for once Yancy's negligence would pay off?" she mused aloud. "Perhaps he did me a favor by not clearing that land."

Ben doubted seriously that the sorry bastard had ever planned it that way.

"It's true what they say about the Lord working in mysterious ways."

"The Lord didn't have much to do with it, Rachel," he contradicted.

She rose from her chair, leaning over the table and brushing his lips with an airy kiss. "Oh, yes he did, Ben. He brought you to this farm at the most crucial time in my life. What's more, he supplied an answer to my problems through you. Those acres of mesquite are no accident, and neither was your timely stopover."

She ruffled his hair and returned to the stove, humming cheerily as she stirred the stew.

He sat stupefied. Could it be that the Almighty had had a hand in this seemingly unrelated series of events? If

180

that were true, then perhaps a miracle would occur and somehow make it possible for him to stay on with Rachel. For in truth, he secretly prayed that he would become a part of her and Meggie's life—not temporarily, but always.

In the remaining days Ben helped her till the fields for winter wheat. God did not intercede as he had hoped, but Ben was blessed by a midnight visit from Rachel at his cubbyhole the night before his planned departure. It was like a dream, and in fact he was unsure the following morning if they had really made love or if the whole experience had been one of his vivid fantasies. The smell of her perfume had been real, though, as had the caress of her lean, smooth body and the velvety texture of her voice as she whispered, "I had to come . . . to thank you for all that you are and all that you've done. Go where you must, but please know that you'll be missed." And yet they had made hazy love in the dark and in aching silence, so in the light of day and in the company of Meggie at breakfast the next morning, he was uncertain if Rachel had actually been in his arms at all.

"When I get home from school today, can we go watch 'em cut down the mesquite s'more, Ben?" Meggie slurped her milk, a white moustache clinging to her upper lip. She had no idea that upon her return from school Ben would be gone from the farm. Coward that he was, he couldn't bring himself to prepare her for his leaving. Instead, he had written her a long and loving letter that he planned to leave on her pillow, asking forgiveness for his sudden departure and telling her how very special she was and that he would never forget her.

Rachel knew of his intent—knew and secretly grieved at the loss she and Meggie were both about to suffer. Her hand shook as she raised the coffee cup to her lips. Damn! Why hadn't he expressed some small regret at leaving? If only he had given her a shred of hope that he might be undecided.

Ben tried to swallow the toast wedged in his throat. A blast of the school bus horn saved him from telling his first and only lie to the child. "Better hurry," he chided, wiping her mouth with a napkin.

She gathered up her books and lunch pail, making a dash for the bus.

He couldn't let a last chance to cuddle her pass. "Meggie," he called after her, beckoning the tot to his side.

"I'm late, and I gotta go, Ben." She wiggled impatiently.

"I know, but come give me a big hug before you do."

He didn't have to ask twice. Meggie ran to him, flinging a free arm around his neck and pressing her cherub cheek to his. "I love you so much, Ben," she declared before bounding out the door.

At the sight of the two clenching, Rachel vaulted from her place at the table and began to blindly go through the motions of scraping the breakfast dishes.

She dropped a favorite piece of pottery, then cursed a blue streak at her clumsiness. He came to her, slipping his arms around her slender waist and kissing her temple. Her heart cried out to be heard, but he missed, or chose not to acknowledge, its plea. "I wish I had the right words for you and her both."

"It's not necessary. I know this is as hard for you as it is for me." She fought back the tears.

"Please reassure Meggie that I care about her very much, and . . ." His voice broke and he relinquished his hold on her.

182

"I will," she said chokingly. "Do you need any help gathering your things?" Her fingers gripped the edge of the sink. She didn't dare to look at him for fear the slim hold she had on herself would crumble at the slightest contact or excuse.

"No. I'm all packed. I just need to collect my duffel bag." He strode from the room, taking this sad memory of her with him to store with all the others.

Feeling as if she were suffocating, she ran onto the back porch to gulp air. She clung to the porch post, gazing at the barren fields through misty eyes. Was this what God intended? Nothing more than the end of Ben and the beginning of winter wheat? Her stomach cramped, and she sank to the steps, feeling weak and praying for strength. If only he had voiced a desire to stay, made one overture that she could interpret as a semicommitment. But he had not. And she would not try to dissuade him from leaving the farm if that was not where he felt he belonged. But it hurt to let him go. It hurt worse than the time Yancy had found her bleeding profusely from a deep machete cut to her shin and had cauterized the wound with a red-hot Bowie knife before rushing her to the clinic in Lubbock. She'd been in shock then and hadn't felt the slice to the bone. This time it was different. This time she was cut to the very core, and the pain registered in every nerve of her body.

She sensed Ben's approach and hastily wiped her eyes. He stood behind the screen door, allowing himself one last glimpse at the woman he loved. Dammit! If only she'd have given him a reason to linger—one significant gesture to let him know she might in time be able to accept him as something more than an intimate friend. Why'd she have to be so damned independent? He wanted to kill Yancy all over again for making her so wary of love.

He caught a firmer grip on his duffel bag, took a last look at the tilled fields that encompassed traces of his sweat, drew a deep breath, and then walked out the door, across the porch, and down the steps.

"All and all, it hasn't been too bad a season, Rachel." He pulled the brim of the Stetson lower over his brow.

She got to her feet, shading her eyes to block out the glare of the autumn sun. If anything, he looked even better than he had on the first day she'd met him. "I'd ask you to write, but I know you'll probably be on the move a lot."

"Probably" was all he answered. "Well, I guess this is it." A muscle tensed in his cheek as he prepared himself for the long, long walk to the road.

"I suppose so." She tightened her legs to quell their shaking.

He nodded her an adieu, quickly pivoting and striking out toward the gate.

She stood as paralyzed as she had been on the day the hailstorm hit. But this time there would be no Ben around to pick up the pieces—no Ben to kiss away her tears—no Ben across the table—no Ben in the fields—no Ben to share the day-to-day joys and trials—no Ben to share her bed. Her life would be so empty without him. She wouldn't be able to stand it. Yet she was doing nothing to prevent it.

He was almost to the gate when she cried out his name and ran after him. "You can't just keep drifting aimlessly, you know. It doesn't matter how far you travel or where you go. You're not going to find peace until you accept yourself." She hadn't the vaguest notion what in the hell she was saying. It only mattered that she had temporarily

184

stayed his exit from her life. "What does it matter what you once achieved and lost? The only thing that counts is here and now and what you stand to gain in the future," she prattled on senselessly, trying her damnedest to dissuade him from leaving and still somehow retain her pride.

He knew she was trying to forestall his departure, but he was unsure why. Torn between wanting to stay under any terms and needing to know he meant something other than just a convenience to her, Ben hesitated.

"You're going to break Meggie's heart," she said desperately.

His own heart constricted at the thought. "Young children have a way of mending quickly." His gaze traveled from her to an oncoming pickup truck, thinking it would be far easier for them both to end this hard parting.

Rachel sensed his urge to escape. Panicked, she blurted, "What can I say to change your mind? Would it make a difference if I told you that you're breaking my heart as well?" There, she had done it! She'd admitted she loved him! Her pulse ceased to beat during the split-second eternity it took for him to respond.

"All the difference in the world, babe. But you have to say what I've waited a whole damned season to hear. I have to know." He would not be satisfied with less than a binding declaration.

"I love you, Ben Eaton. As God's my witness, I truly do." Devotion shimmered in her almond eyes.

The duffel bag dropped to the ground, and he gathered her into his aching arms with a surrendering shudder. "I would've come back eventually," he whispered, his calloused hands slipping through the silk of her hair.

She tilted her head back and cast him a saucy look.

"Well, of course you would've. Only a fool would walk off without collecting his back wages."

Collect he did—claiming her lips and a first installment on a blissful life as his ride out of Mesquite Junction chugged on by.

EPILOGUE

Several seasons had come and gone since Bubba Atkins gave Bennett Earl Eaton a lift to the widow Daniels's farm. Once again, Bubba was toting a hitchhiker up the blacktopped road and supplying unsolicited local color to pass the time.

"Almost planting time again. Pretty soon these empty fields will be bloomin' with cotton. If this fine weather holds out, I expect it might be a fairly decent season."

The stranger yawned and counted the miles to Lubbock.

"Up yonder is the Eaton place. They're nice enough folk, but kinda peculiar. She's always smiling, like someone who ain't got a care in the world. And he's into computerized farmin'. Damnedest thing I ever heard of. As best I understand it, he feeds a bunch a facts and figures into this electronic thing, and it projects his yield. It ain't natural, but dat-blamed if that farm ain't turnin' a profit whilst the rest of us barely scrimp by."

The bored hiker lit up a smoke and wondered if the old man was ever going to shut up.

As the backfiring pickup passed by a group of children playing stickball in the yard, Bubba stuck his head out the window and gave a friendly holler. "Yo! Meggie. How's Ben, Jr.'s croup?"

She motioned to the cooing toddler in the buggy. "He's fine now, Bubba. It was only his teething. He got two new ones just last week. Daddy Ben says he'll be eating corn on the cob by summer."

"Wouldn't surprise me," Bubba chuckled, ducking his head back inside and accelerating up the road.

"Rachel and Ben got themselves a pair of great kids. It's no wonder they don't miss a Sunday service. Yes, sir, they're mighty blessed. 'Course, there was a time when Ben wasn't too keen on God, but that's another story."

The hitchhiker was counting his own blessings, thinking that the windy farmer was about to desist the jabber.

But Bubba was just warming up, and the stranger would know the life story of practically every individual who resided in the community before he reached Lubbock. Unlike Ben Eaton, this hitchhiker would not be lingering. In fact, the stranger wondered to himself what would possess a man to want to stop over in the podunk town. But of course, he hadn't been sidetracked by a pretty widow in distress or known a bittersweet season that fostered a deep and abiding love.

Now you can reserve December's
Candlelights
<u>before</u> they're published!

♥ You'll have copies set aside for *you*
the instant they come off press.

♥ You'll save yourself precious shopping
time by arranging for *home delivery.*

♥ You'll feel proud and efficient about
organizing a system that *guarantees* delivery.

♥ You'll avoid the disappointment of not
finding *every* title you want and need.

ECSTASY SUPREMES $2.75 each

☐ **149 TODAY AND ALWAYS,** Alison Tyler 18688-9
☐ **150 THE NIGHT OF HIS LIFE,** Blair Cameron 16396-X
☐ **151 MURPHY'S CHARM,** Linda Randall Wisdom 16201-7
☐ **152 IN THE HEAT OF THE SUN,** Anne Silverlock 14134-6

ECSTASY ROMANCES $2.25 each

☐ **474 REBEL LOVE,** Anna Hudson 17413-9
☐ **475 A WIFE FOR RANSOM,** Pat West 19684-1
☐ **476 EDEN'S SPELL,** Heather Graham 12224-4
☐ **477 TO TAME A MAN,** Rose Marie Ferris 18502-5
☐ **478 THE SCOUNDREL'S KISS,** Joan Grove 17641-7
☐ **479 TUG OF WAR,** Lori Copeland 19021-5
☐   **9 *SURRENDER BY MOONLIGHT,*** Bonnie Drake . . . 18426-6
☐   **20 *THE FACE OF LOVE,*** Anne N. Reisser 12496-4

 At your local bookstore or use this handy coupon for ordering:

Dell **DELL READERS SERVICE—DEPT. B1301A**
6 REGENT ST., LIVINGSTON, N.J. 07039

Please send me the above title(s) I am enclosing $ _____ (please add 75¢ per copy to cover
postage and handling) Send check or money order—no cash or CODs Please allow 3-4 weeks for shipment

Ms./Mrs./Mr _____

Address _____

City/State _____ Zip _____